ONLY

IF

WE'RE

CAUGHT

ONLY

IF

WE'RE

CAUGHT

stories

THERESSA SLIND

Thistledown
Press

Thistledown Press Ltd.
P.O. Box 30105 Westview
Saskatoon, SK S7L 7M6
www.thistledownpress.com

Library and Archives Canada Cataloguing in Publication
Title: Only if we're caught / Theressa Slind.
Other titles: Only if we are caught
Names: Slind, Theressa, author.
Description: Short stories.
Identifiers: Canadiana 20210185082 | ISBN 9781771872119 (softcover)
Classification: LCC PS8637.L53 O55 2021 | DDC C813/.6—dc23

Cover and book design by Natalie Olsen, Kisscut Design
Cover images © InnaPoka and ArtHeart/Shuterstock.com
Printed and bound in Canada

Thistledown Press gratefully acknowledges the financial assistance
of The Canada Council for the Arts, SK Arts, and the government of
Canada for its publishing program.

 Canada

for Travis and Kate

CONTENTS

THEIR
FEVER DREAMS
WERE CHILD
DRAWINGS

9

But, oh, sweetness. The hallway where she waits in her wheelchair is painted the colour of cookie dough, which she used to eat by the spoonful. Her weakness for baking had softened a sturdy, farm-wife frame. She used to take up more space. But her current bird-lightness, her porous-boned spine curling in on itself as if to tuck beak under wing for sleep, has its advantages. She sees things differently — sideways — and memories lend texture, so the first sight of the little girl in William's old room is paired with the smell and taste of brown sugar, butter, and vanilla.

The girl is lying on her belly at the foot of William's old bed, concentrating on a drawing. Margaret waits for William out of habit alone. He died last week and she misses his teasing: *Maggie, darling, let me get a word in, will you?* — because Parkinson's has left her speechless — or *Giving me the silent treatment again, I see.* The other Aspen Grove residents thought of them as going steady.

The room's new occupant is Caroline, according to the nameplate beside the doorway. In a niche below the nameplate is a soapstone carving of a whale. William called it his personality niche, and only last week it was bursting with tamer pieces from his collection of seventeenth-century Japanese erotica. She worried over this affectation during her first few months at Aspen Grove, obsessing over which of her knickknacks really said *Margaret*. She gave up after watching her temporary neighbours' rotating display of gewgaws. Her personality niche is an anonymous crypt for one dead fly.

The girl looks up at her and trails snot along her sleeve. She has dark hair in pillow-fuzzed braids and big brown eyes. How old would she be? Margaret waves.

The girl holds up four fingers and says, "Actually, four and a half."

Having reached her ninety-third year, Margaret is not surprised. *This is how it is now* is her reaction to everything from cellphones to the accountant's neck tattoo to telepathic children.

"What's that, Pyper?" A woman's voice from deeper in the room, hidden from view. Pyper, as a proper name, is unfamiliar to Margaret, but she likes it: girl Pyper, sandpiper, Pied Piper, icing piper, sweetness.

"I wasn't talking to you, Mama." Girl Pyper wriggles into a cross-legged position. "I was talking to Margaret." Pyper points. Mama pokes her head around the doorway, offers a rigid smile.

"We'll let Nana sleep," says Mama to Pyper.

Nice to let Caroline sleep, thinks Margaret. There are good and natural reasons for their collective fatigue. Practice for the Big Sleep, for one.

"Mama, what's the Big Sleep? It sounds more fun than my little sleeps."

"Quit talking silly, Pyper. Let's find a playground."

"Yay!" Pyper bunny-hops out of the room and holds onto the wheelchair. "You're funny," she whispers.

Margaret cups her ear, trapping the child's warm breath as, sideways, she watches the pair leave. Who is this Pyper? Compensation for losing William? Life's answer to overstaying its welcome? *I know it's miserable, Margaret. Here, take this. Now quit whining.* She lifts her bird legs off their footrests and lets her heavy white sneakers drop to the floor with a squeak. She paddles away, gliding along the shimmering, polished floor, as silent as a swan. Or maybe a duck or goose. Mustn't let life's gifts go to one's head.

When Pyper and Mama wheel Caroline into the activity room the next morning, Margaret is parked along with her fellow residents in a ragged semicircle. She rubs thumb against fingers excitedly.

Pyper crawls onto Mama's lap, calls across the room, "Hi, Margaret."

Margaret lifts a hand and imagines her old smile, wide and dimpling. She is relieved, for Pyper's sake, to see the Nice Exercise Lady, not the I-Picked-the-Wrong-Career Exercise Lady, take her seat at the top of the semicircle and say, "Let's get started, friends. Shoulders, everyone. Shoulders back, shoulders forward. Look! Even the little girl is doing it. What's your name, pet?"

"Pyper."

"Pardon me, sweetheart? Up, down, that's right."

"Pyper! With a *Y!*"

"Let's stretch our necks. Turn and look at your neighbour to the right, now to the left. Let's show little Pyper-with-a-*Y* how we do it! Pyper, dear, are you sick? Cough into your elbow. Like this." The most obedient residents bring the crook of their elbows up to their faces, following along with the exercise.

Afterwards, though Manfred has fallen asleep in his wheelchair (a blessing), Margaret and most of the others have an extra, theoretical, spring in their step. Pyper slides off Mama's lap and plays on an imaginary high wire in the middle of the semicircle, placing one foot in front of the other with her arms straight out at her sides. "Whoa, whoa!" and she goes flying off her high wire. In those residents like Margaret left with only one bland expression, the glee is hard to detect, but many can still speak.

"What an angel."

"How clever. Aren't you a darling."

"Clover wouldn't have approved, but I say better seen *and* heard."

Margaret feels a new sense of solidarity with her fellow residents. Better to think of them fondly as a group, rather than as beloved individuals. William would be her last beloved individual. Other than Pyper, of course.

"Pyper, time to go." Mama stands. "Say bye-bye."

Pyper skips over and places her warm hand on Margaret's, resting tremulously in her lap. "Bye, Margaret. William sounds nice."

Mama gives her a puzzled frown. Margaret would smile to reassure her if she could.

Pyper visits Aspen Grove with her mama every morning for a week. They flew in on a plane – Pyper isn't sure from where, but they speak English there – and are staying in a hotel. Pyper swims in the pool and goes down the waterslide a thousand hundred times each afternoon. "Nana is like Mama's Mama," is how Pyper explains the relationship. So Pyper and Mama study the activity board each morning and wheel Caroline to *Words! Words! Words!* and *Folding Laundry!* and *CBC News!* They accompany Caroline to lunch. "This smooshy corn is delicious," Pyper says. "Can we make green Jell-O at home, Mama?"

Margaret becomes a real joiner that week, participating in even the most inane activities, and, with Pyper in the dining room, she cleans her plate, fighting through tiresome swallowing, imagining William's wry commentary: *A moment on the lips, a lifetime on the hips, darling.* And William isn't the only one who comes back to her. In some lucid dream, her long-dead husband, Jack, spends an afternoon reminiscing about their time together before the children were born, about the house they built on the farm, scrambling to get the exterior walls up before the snow fell, and sleeping, eating, and loving in their framed but unfinished interior. From their lumpy bed under three layers of quilts, they could see clear across the house to the kitchen sink, a deep back-breaker salvaged from the old farmhouse. She was never cold in that house, but her back often ached.

One morning the music therapist doesn't show up for *Chris Sings Bing!*, so Pyper and Mama's improvised activity is pushing Caroline in laps around the cookie-dough hallways. Mama tries to stop Pyper from going into Margaret's room, but her favourite aide, Abby, happens to be passing by and tells Mama not to worry, a visit from a child is "better than pet therapy." Abby winks and Mama looks doubtful.

"I heard your cough, Margaret," says Pyper, "so I knew this was your room. Why don't you have any pretty things beside your door?"

Margaret thinks about what her empty personality niche must say to Pyper.

"You're not empty, Margaret."

Would you decorate it for me?

And the dead fly gets company: a lifelike stick-figure drawing of Margaret.

By the end of the week, her niche holds a collection of drawings on pastel-coloured paper the same texture as her skin. Her niche features airplanes, farmyards, cats, and other residents: Manfred sleeping in his wheelchair, Caroline eating soup. Pyper explains her drawings, fidgeting at Margaret's side, picking at a bit of loose rubber on her armrest. "Look. Nana spills like me. That's a blob of potato soup on her bib."

I love your drawings, Pyper, and I love you. What are those?

"Those are wings, Margaret. You're flying. I'm flying too. That's me. And your wheelchair is flying." Pyper sneezes messily. "Mama says we fly home tomorrow. Okay, bye. Love you too."

Margaret is sicker. She feels hot for the first time in years and lies in bed for two days while Jack, at the farmhouse sink, dampens a cloth to cool her forehead. And, oh, sweetness. William bakes cookies for the three of them and cracks wise: *Quel ménage. Aren't we twenty-first century?* Margaret loves and is loved, and she dreams along with her fellow Aspen Grove residents. Their fever dreams are child drawings of figures flying through the air with grace, like ducks, geese, swans.

AMYGDULE

A frigid wind careens off granite headstones and smooth, dark basalt rock that surface around the perimeter of the cemetery like a pod of prehistoric whales. Ben has worked at the funeral home all his adult life, finally taking it over from his father five years ago, but the rock surrounding the cemetery has been here forever and still reveals new colours and contours depending on the light and weather, always suggests new similes. He sees whales today.

The wind stings as he walks towards his favourite bench and listens to McFadden school young Kevin. He's learned more about the area's geological underpinnings in the three weeks since the geologist died than he has during the rest of his forty-three years living in the mining town. McFadden is his new ghost and a serious pain in the ass, and he still doesn't know what the old guy needs from him.

Almost everyone uses granite for headstones these days, son, but if I had to choose my own monument I'd go for quartzite, a metamorphic rock composed mainly of... Can you guess, Kevin?

Quartz!

That's right, quartz. And metamorphic rock is...

Rock that's been altered by extreme heat or pressure or chemical processes.

Very good, Kevin.

And oh, Mr. McFadden. Kevin raises his hand as if in class. *Quartzite is a non-foliated metamorphic rock. It was originally sandstone.*

Today, like every day, Kevin wears a white and orange patterned shirt with snaps up the front and a spearpoint collar. His shaggy hair could have been the style at the time he died, but Ben is pretty sure it's the product of parental neglect. Kevin has been six since 1982, the year he went missing to everyone but his classmate. At six, Ben already knew what missing meant – his mother had been missing from his life since she died the previous winter, leaving a hole in the centre of his existence – so he didn't know what the fuss was about. He'd say to the adults, "But Kevin's right here. Beside me. Right here." Eventually, he came to understand that no one else could see Kevin and that Kevin was dead, like his mother but only sort of.

Well done, Kevin, says McFadden. *Quartzite is highly durable, attractive – expensive, mind you. My own son chose Blue Pearl granite from Norway. Wouldn't have been my pick, but he didn't have much choice, did he, given granite's all this guy sources.*

Ben's granite offerings are industry standard, and he doesn't appreciate being referred to as "this guy" so often.

"You could've made pre-arrangements, McFadden. People do that, you know."

Funeral directors, bunch of crooks. Could just bundle us in a sack and throw us in a hole. Dust to dust. Instead –

He ignores this part of the lecture as he reaches his regular bench, a memorial to one of the town's founding prospectors. He's wearing McFadden's parka which is proving a superior smoking garment: ugly, beige, roomy, pocket rich. The zipper of his previous parka – designed and priced for Everest – broke within a year and the hi-tech fabric was dotted with ember burns by the time he incinerated it along with McFadden.

It seemed like a fair trade. Trouble is, McFadden always appears with it either bundled under his arm or slung casually over a shoulder. Ben isn't worried about the old guy being burdened with the piece of junk for all eternity. Rather, it reminds him of the basic transactional nature of their relationship.

Other than Kevin, his ghosts come and go. Go after he helps them in some way. Some of the ghosts are coy about what they need, like McFadden; others are direct. The first thing Conrad said to Ben was, *I need to talk to her,* and he never shut up about his wife. Though Ben wouldn't pass along any messages directly – his business couldn't withstand gossip about the funeral director who communed with ghosts – he agreed to bring Conrad close. So he shovelled snow off the widow's driveway and mowed her lawn, while Conrad got whatever it was off his chest. These ghosts are tethered to Ben by some physical law as compelling as gravity, and they are lucky to be tethered to a loser with so much free time on his hands. He has no wife, no family, no kids, no girlfriend, few friends. And he still has no idea what McFadden needs.

"What am I going to have to do for this parka?" he mumbles, a cigarette between his lips, patting his pockets for a lighter, interrupting McFadden's flow.

Always the drama with you young people, says McFadden, peering over his reading glasses, perpetually halfway down his nose at withering level. Ben wishes he'd tossed them before cremation.

"Forty-three is young?"

Seems forty-three's the new thirteen.

"Maybe you're right. I still love smoking, *Super Mario,* the *Star Wars* franchise –"

Grow up. Kevin is more mature than you.

Ben finds the lighter in a left breast pocket — though it feels like something else — and lights the cigarette, cupping his hand around the vulnerable flame.

Smoking is bad for you. Mr. McFadden said so.

"I know, Kevin." He takes a second drag. "When you grow up you can make your own poor choices."

McFadden covers the boy's ears. *No need to rub it in,* he scolds Ben. The old ghost lets go of Kevin's head and addresses the boy with great seriousness. *Kevin, listen to me. Dead is best. Remember that. The living are a bunch of shits. It's a marvel he's even using the parka, given his throwaway culture.*

McFadden died while ice fishing near his winterized cabin and was sitting frozen in a lawn chair watching his tip-ups with clouded eyes when the conservation officer found him. It took two days to thaw him, but he adapted as easily as Ben had ever seen to his new incorporeal state, instantly adopting an us (dead) versus them (living) position. Like he was relieved not to be part of the problem anymore. Ben gets the appeal, given the garbage state of macro affairs, and he's glad Kevin has a new companion to tutor him in geology and contemporary attitudes towards smoking. A grandpa to complement Ben, his ersatz big-brother-dad.

Ben pats his breast pocket again. The nicotine has yanked a memory thread, and he pursues the thing he felt there earlier. Yes, there is something else in the breast pocket; not in the outside pocket where he retrieved his lighter, but behind it. He undoes the parka's top two snaps, reaches into the inside breast pocket, and pulls out a folded piece of paper.

There's Alice! Here she comes! Kevin bobs with excitement.

He doesn't seem to care what Ben has found. In this moment, he only cares about Alice, who works for Ben at the funeral home.

Christ, you found it. McFadden, on the other hand, is fidgeting, moving the ruined hi-tech parka from one arm to the other, then putting it on. It's too small and bunches up his suit jacket around his neck. Let him stew a bit. Ben's excited to see Alice too, though he plays it a bit cooler than Kevin.

Alice arrives in an eddy of formaldehyde, her voice barely audible over the wind. "I need a smoke."

She doesn't smoke, but her versatility is one of the things Ben loves about her. Would she mind draining poor Mr. Williams who'd been found a little late? "I likes my men ripe." Cleaning up the barf in the chapel? "Stomach contents of the living? What a treat!" Fixing the website? "Millennial to the rescue!" What would he do without her?

He glances behind him, towards the funeral home. Kevin has slipped his hand into Alice's and is staring up at her adoringly. Ben isn't jealous – Alice is clearly a superior person – but he feels sorry for the boy. Kevin can play around Alice, who is unaware she has a worshipful ghost, but only when Ben is close. The physics of the dead is limiting.

"Give me one of those," she says. "Mrs. Chan's bedsores were not pretty." She shifts from one foot to the other, hugging herself against the cold, and perches on the edge of the bench. Kevin bounces gleefully on her jouncing knee. Alice is never still. Ben can't figure how she ever settles down enough to sleep and imagines her bound, sexily, in a tourniquet of bedding after a night of constant rolling. Then he feels ashamed of this thought and makes a show of getting a cigarette for her.

"What've you got there, boss?" She points at the folded paper in his hand.

Just throw it away, says McFadden.

"Don't know," he says through lips clamped down on two cigarettes and raises an eyebrow at McFadden who is chewing on a hangnail. Ben lights a cigarette for Alice and hands it to her.

Alice, stop! Smoking is bad for you!

Ben's careless flame ignited the corner of the paper, but the wind extinguishes it in a moment. When he unfolds the paper, the edges are brown and scalloped. "It's a fishing licence."

"It's a map. *X* marks the spot." Alice points at the *X* in the middle of the page. "Arrgh." She squeezes her left eye shut and makes a hook out of her right hand. "Thar's gold methinks, matey." Kevin laughs. She puffs on the cigarette without inhaling.

Indeed, superimposed over the faint and copious legal rights and responsibilities of a Manitoba fisherman is what looks like a treasure map. It's drawn in a firm but shaky hand with thick carpenter's pencil, as if dashed off urgently while McFadden was having a stroke. *X* does mark a spot, with Hwy. 10 a distance from it. Thin, trailing lines from the highway leading to it. Longitudinal coordinates. The initials JGM in the corner. John Garvey McFadden.

"Do you think McFadden drew it out on the lake before he died?" asks Alice.

Yes, says McFadden.

"Maybe," says Ben.

I don't know what I was thinking putting that in writing. What would Brendan do with it?

Brendan is McFadden's son who chose the Blue Pearl granite headstone. At the funeral Brendan wept openly. Ben rarely sees men get as broken up. He doesn't want to think about the level of emotion he showed at his own father's funeral. Too much? Too little? He was too preoccupied by Mrs. Thiessen, who'd died while making jelly, and her overweening need to know if the jelly had set, to properly experience the thing. Is the map a key to Brendan's inheritance? McFadden had been a geologist scout for gold companies in his day. There'd always been rumours around town about his worth. A treasure chest full of gold would allow Ben to raise Alice's salary and to keep Funerals R Us from circling his business — his inheritance — like a pack of corporate zombies. More importantly, though, he senses this is what McFadden needs from him.

"Ben?" says Alice. "You should call his son."

Don't call him. I made a mistake. I was having a bloody stroke.

Alice snaps her fingers. "Ben? Are you there? Call the son, I said." She springs from the bench. "Back to work. Mrs. Chan isn't going to embalm herself."

Ahhh, Alice, whines Kevin. *Don't go.*

Ben doesn't want Alice to go either. He wants to talk this through with her, but of course he can't. Should he send the treasure map to Brendan? It's tempting because that's the last thing McFadden wants, but he knows he has to keep it, find the treasure — whatever it is — if he's ever going to get rid of the guy. He pictures himself with an eye patch and sword, chest out on a swaying galleon. He'll have to wait for the ground to thaw.

Ben's spade sinks into the sandy soil with a familiar *thock*. The *X* on McFadden's map led to a patch of land, cleared of pine maybe ten years ago and now home to a wild blueberry patch and a shitload of mosquitoes who create a menacing hum. He reapplies the layer of repellent he has sweated off and lights a cigarette.

He's been at it on and off for two months and is starting to feel less like a pirate and more like a crazy person. With his metal detector so far he's found machine parts, saw teeth, aluminum beer cans, and other essential tools of the logging crew. He knows he can't afford this treasure hunt, but neither can he stop, because, though he doubts he'll find gold, he knows he'll find something. If he possesses no other skills, he possesses this: a sensitivity to messages from secret places. He's on the way to resolving McFadden's problem, whatever it is, and then he'll be rid of him. The old ghost is reaching peak annoying, having, with characteristic alacrity, long become comfortable with the treasure hunt. Plus, the fucker still hasn't said what they're looking for. *All in due time*, he'll say maddeningly when Ben demands to know. He'll cite research that demonstrates delayed satisfaction results in a happier life and that Ben should enjoy the process: nature, exercise, quality time with Kevin. *I wish I'd spent more time with Brendan.*

But Kevin is acting strangely. Ever since Ben started digging in the blueberry patch, Kevin's been mopey and distant. At first he thought it was because Alice wasn't around, but now he isn't so sure. Kevin routinely retreats to the top of a pine tree or curls up in the truck bed or buzzes around the perimeter of the clearing in endless laps.

Ben steps on his spent cigarette and continues roving with his metal detector and digging, overseen by McFadden, sitting cross-legged on an outcropping of rock. The old jacket in his lap.

Flow-banded rhyolite — note the unusually large amygdule, Ben. Here, by my feet. Ben.

"What's an amygdule?" He doesn't ask out of curiosity; he asks because McFadden won't stop pestering until he admits he doesn't know what an amygdule is. Also, he wants to perk Kevin up, because he knows Kevin will have the answer. Kevin has always been the better student, feeding Ben the correct answers in class throughout all his schooling. He knows all Ben knows, and more. And yet Kevin is still a child, innocent in many ways — would rather play than do anything else, always hides in a closet or drawer during Ben's rare moments of intimacy with women. He wishes his ghosts were all so reticent. Would make these moments less rare.

Kevin, McFadden shouts. *Tell dumb-dumb what an amygdule is.*

Kevin's voice is not perky, but he answers the question from his perch in a nearby pine. *A deposit of minerals found in igneous rock. The minerals fill a cavity left in the rock from gas bubbles that formed as the lava cooled.*

Thank you, Kevin. Your youthfulness is contagious. I haven't been able to sit cross-legged since fifth grade. Look how flexible I've become.

"You just don't feel pain anymore because you're dead." Ben swats a mosquito on his cheek. "Nothing to be proud of."

Poor Ben. Psychic pain is the worst. I like her, you know.

"What are we talking about?"

Alice. Why don't you ask her out on a date?

"She's my employee."

Do you have a harassment policy or something?

"No."

Well.

"She's not interested."

The living are so tiresome. Why do you think she still works for you at that death factory? Open your eyes. You didn't notice the fiddleheads at the edge of the forest either and now they're gone. I saw them for ten bucks a dozen at the Forks last spring. You're blind to opportunities.

It's true Ben doesn't know why Alice works for him, but is he blind to opportunities? He exists in a state of perpetual distraction as his ghosts carry on their own business with him no matter if he's watching a movie, at a party, running a funeral service, engaging in sex, or digging for buried treasure. He thinks of himself as a functioning schizophrenic – which he feels is pretty good given the circumstances – but where does that leave fiddleheads? Alice? Undisturbed.

The metal detector starts beeping frantically.

Out of the corner of his eye, he sees Kevin swoop down from his tree and duck behind a squat Scotch pine. McFadden drifts over, his legs still folded in a yogic pose. Ben starts digging with greater hope and care than usual. His ghosts know something. He scrapes at the sandy soil, easily uprooting some small blueberry bushes and pine and aspen seedlings, stirring up the smell of pine forest and earth. He feels its relative cool on his hot face. A Matchbox car – a rusted but recognizable Camaro – settles on top of a pile of soil. Kevin rushes to the toy car, gets onto his hands and knees, and starts making engine noises. Ben scrapes off another layer of soil, reaches down, and picks up a white object, the rubber sole and toe cap of a child's running shoe. Much of the canvas rotted away. He turns it over in his hand and something falls out of it and drops beside the toy. A tiny bone. A phalange.

There you are, says McFadden.

There I am, says Kevin.

Ben looks back and forth between Kevin and McFadden. The mosquitoes' hum roars in his ears. His heartbeat thrums along the spade handle.

Keep digging, says McFadden. *Gently.*

With shaky arms, Ben slowly uncovers the remains of a child. Some rotted clothing clings to the skeleton, the exaggerated points of a collar, the plastic tabs poking through. A row of rusty snaps. He's panicky and short of breath. The sweat on his skin cools, feels like cling wrap. He fumbles in his pocket for his phone even though he knows there's no service.

They'll think you did it.

"Me?"

Yes, you. Look at yourself.

He looks down at his filthy T-shirt, spade, and metal detector to see if it all adds up to murderer, and he sees that it does. The appearance of guilt makes him feel guilty and chilled by a fresh sheath of sweat. But, wait, he was six when Kevin died. They'd date the remains, identify the body. He'd still have to admit how he got the map, which was basically theft of a decedent's effects. He'd lose his licence, his business, Alice. And, despite his innocence, people would associate him with child killing. Alice would associate him with child killing. And not just any child. Kevin. How is Kevin feeling about this? How had he felt? How could Ben be thinking about himself at a time like this? He looks up. Kevin is zooming around the site with his hands at ten and two, spitting the sounds of a v8 engine, downshifting, spinning out. He shouts, *You found it, Ben! Thank you!* Ben reaches down and pockets the dirt-packed toy.

Through the fog of shock, he remembers it was McFadden's map. McFadden knew what he'd find in the wild blueberry patch and is hovering with his eyes closed and hands clasped behind his back, shaking his head slightly.

"What the living fuck, McFadden!"

Take it easy now.

"How am I supposed to do that?"

McFadden raises his shaggy eyebrows and looks over his reading glasses.

Ben drops onto his knees, gestures towards Kevin's remains. "I don't want to know this." And he doesn't, hasn't ever. How is it he's never asked Kevin what happened to him? Why has Kevin never volunteered the information? Why hasn't he thought Kevin might need something from him too? Why is he the only ghost who's stuck around? Has Kevin been protecting him from the truth all these years? Sparing him the knowledge? He grinds a handful of soil between his palms, seeing but not feeling McFadden put a hand on his shoulder.

Beautiful soil.

"What?"

Soil's perfect for blueberry bushes. Acidic. Good drainage because of the sand. Soil mechanics. Look how it crumbles in your hands. Does it feel gritty? You know, I miss that. The feel of things. As much as I hate to admit it, you're right, Ben, death is nothing to be proud of. Now I'm pure energy, there's no matter. I flow through. But if Kevin had been pure energy instead of stubborn matter, he wouldn't have been your constant companion.

Ben scoops up another handful of dirt, waits. Kevin is completely absorbed in his pretend Camaro.

Kevin was one of, what, five kids who lived next door? Running wild around the neighbourhood at all hours. Always outside, is my guess, because when they were inside they got screamed at. Terrible people, his parents.

One of the only times Ben visited Kevin's house was for a birthday party, but there wasn't a cake or candles. After playing inside with Kevin's Matchbox cars, the small group of boys was instructed to *Shut the fuck up. Go to the fucking park or something.*

One night, my son Brendan was driving home from a hockey game. Almost in the driveway, and he hit Kevin who'd run out onto the street after something or other. Right outside our house. It was an accident, of course, but Brendan had this scholarship lined up in the States. He was leaving the next week. And the neighbours, the police were always at their door ... I'd done some scouting around here, so this is where I brought Kevin.

"How could you?"

I'm hoping I won't have to keep asking myself that question for all eternity. The living are shits, I told you that. And I was the king of shits, but now I'm trying to make it right. Kevin needs me; I need him; we need you. You need us, it seems. We're bound together.

In a tourniquet? Ben is reminded of the stubborn matter of Alice and her binding sheets as he worries the soil in his hands. It feels gritty. He wonders at the privilege of matter over energy. The world of matter is his advantage, is his to know and feel. The world of pure energy, the world the ghosts inhabit, is his to observe. But does he need the ghosts as McFadden suggests? He can hardly remember a time before Kevin. Maybe Kevin only appeared in grade one because Ben lost his mother and was lonely. Is lonely. Maybe Kevin and the others are not the cause of his loneliness, but an answer to it, a distraction from it. Maybe to the dead his stink of neediness is irresistible. A cavity waiting for mineral fill.

During that night's sliver of northern summer darkness, Ben runs his first funeral service without distractions. Under a sky weighted with stars, he prepares a narrow grave next to McFadden's at the edge of the cemetery where the basalt formation rises highest. He gently lays Kevin's remains, wrapped in McFadden's parka with the Matchbox car in a pocket, into the grave, nestling him next to ancient, unsurprised rock. When this is done, he and McFadden take turns telling stories about Kevin, leaning against the still sun-warmed rock. Kevin crouches on McFadden's headstone, laughing with a child's nostalgia about his own recent past. When the talk has gone on long enough, he starts to get antsy, and McFadden turns to the rock, moves his hand over the surface.

Basalt, feldspar-phyric, some brecciation. Just imagine it, Kevin. The earth's plates shift, collide. Boom! A volcanic sequence is set in motion. A submarine volcano erupts, spewing liquid basalt into the water.

Boom! Splush! Kevin invents the sounds of plate tectonics and underwater volcanoes.

You've got it, son. The water's so cold the top layer of lava hardens quickly, but an underlying flow continues to creep along. And this flow is powerful enough to break off bigger solidified chunks from above which reheat and stretch like Silly Putty, folding in and over themselves. As the lava cools, mineral crystals form, and the whole mass of liquid rock creeps along, cooling, cooling until one day, it stops cold. It's become its monumental, mineral-pitted, crystallized self. Transformed.

Whoa. Kevin hops off the headstone and looks up at McFadden with love. *Watch me.*

Sure thing, kiddo.

While Kevin takes a last spin in his Camaro around the cemetery under McFadden's attentive eye, Ben fills the grave and pieces together patches of turf on top. He lays out a picnic blanket, pours three whiskys, drinks them all, and lies back on the blanket. The northern lights flit across the sky while he enjoys a smoke, and McFadden comments from a distance, *Another perfect night. Consider sharing these with someone, Ben.*

Vroom, vroom, says Kevin as he zooms overhead. *He means Alice!*

When Ben wakes in the cool, damp dawn, his ghosts are gone. Behind a squirrel's insistent scolding, a crow caws from the tallest pine and a high-flying hawk shrieks. The cemetery is alive and so is he. He can tell by how much his body and his heart hurt. At the same time, he feels the giddiness and freedom of having the beloved but irksome relatives leave after an extended stay. He can be himself again. But what is that? What is he without them?

He sits up, then stands, slowly pushing himself off the basalt wall that rises beside him. The rock face is cold now and it seems to shift beneath his hand. He feels dizzy. Or maybe it's the other way around. What would it feel like to turn from a liquid to a solid? How had the basalt felt when it didn't flow anymore? Stuck or strong? Trapped or settled? The ghosts might know. They've already gone from matter to energy, then from energy to, what, matter again? He should have asked them what to expect of the coming folding and faulting sequence.

TUESDAY, MONDAY

Natalie and her friends wore stiff neon vests like sandwich boards advertising their faith in finding Bettina, the little girl who'd wandered into the bush three days ago. This was their second time through the same field because Morgan had a "good feeling." There were hundreds of volunteers, mostly locals, but also people from neighbouring provinces who'd responded to help in the search. Four abreast, they stepped through the ripe wheat, and had to shout to hear one another over the wind. Natalie's vest flared out over her belly, and her ankles swelled further with clingy chickweed. Her friends actually thought they were going to find the girl alive, and she'd give them a big hug or something. Like there wasn't another possibility.

There were possibilities aplenty. A year ago, Natalie's possibilities were few but brilliant: highest graduating mark in school division, scholarship to university, medical school, residency, specialty residency, fulfilling relationship with architect, children optional, half-marathons, wine appreciation, minimally decorated rooms, world travel. All this before thirty. Instead, Andy-fucking-Gustafson: boy she'd gone to school with since kindergarten, boy who'd hilariously rubbed a powdery marshmallow on his butt in grade five, boy who'd grown disastrously irresistible.

Sweat trickled down the aching arch of her lower back into the waistband of her maternity leggings, creating a kind of wet girdle. Uncomfortable, for sure, but better than canning tomatoes with her mother whose disappointment was as thick and scalding as the steam billowing off the canner.

She knew Bettina was dead. Knew it like she knew Tuesday came after Monday. She dragged her feet out at the end of the field, shrugged off the vest.

"We'll find her tomorrow," said Katie. "She'll be so happy to see me. I'm her favourite babysitter."

"You've said." Natalie kicked the chickweed off her ankles.

"Natalie-Fellatalie!" said Christian. "Want a ride home?"

"I'll walk, but, here, take this." She handed him the vest. "I can't spend another minute with World's Greatest Babysitter." The truth of it was carried away on the wind along with the thought that soon she might need a babysitter.

"Bettina passed through this field," shouted Morgan from the car. "I just know it."

The sun was low and blinding. The weight on Natalie's pelvis made her legs feel squashed. She already regretted turning down the ride, but there was no way she was going to chase after them, and she couldn't turn back time: not one minute, not eight and a half months. She called out, "And I don't collect stamps anymore, Christian."

Their old joke suddenly sounded stale, and she heard Katie's unmistakable "Awkward," as she waddled up from the ditch onto the gravel road. She inhaled the dust kicked up by the departing car. Then a red truck with an out-of-province licence plate sped by in the direction of her parents' farm, fishtailing to a stop half a kilometre away. A man jumped out and ran into the bush bordering a harvested field. Whatever. People were acting weird these days.

She yarded on her leggings and started walking along the side of the road, checking her dead phone for a message from Andy. He was harvesting with his dad, making an effort to learn the business so he could "support the baby" after he graduated. He actually had a plan, but the thought of living in the old farmhouse Andy's family normally rented to their hired men made her want to cry. For one, she was pretty sure that is where she'd gotten pregnant. Two, it was disgusting – there were mouse droppings even in the tub. Three, the faded *Playboy* calendar stuck on September 1987 Playmate of the Month, Gwen Hajek. In that old farmhouse she would become as stuck in time as poor, naked Gwen.

There were no other vehicles in sight apart from the parked truck ahead, so she moved to the middle of the road, keeping to one of the two worn tire tracks. She felt every stone through her mom's retro, thin-soled volleyball shoes. The irony. She was literally walking a mile in her mother's shoes.

There were things to admire, sure. Her mother worked angry, but, holy shit: the house and yard were spotless, bread was homemade, church and town committees were rigorously chaired, school lunches were envied, farm product was managed to the highest organic standards, local kids were schooled in Royal Conservatory. All done with a rigid dash for a mouth and quotation mark creases between her eyes. One time Katie said Natalie should cheer up unless she wanted "resting bitch face like your mom." Better than resting dumb face like Katie's mother.

Last night after supper Natalie had found her mother on the computer, tracing a finger down the screen.

"Mom, that's why the screen gets so dirty. Just highlight a column." She reached for the mouse.

"Stop it. I know what to do." Her mother always knew what to do, and to their running argument she added, "Yes, I am certain now. You will stay home and finish high school online while I take care of the baby."

"Studies show face-to-face instruction is thirty-five percent more effective than online."

"Not when instruction is provided face-to-face by Gavin Prescott. You're better off at home. That man can't tie his shoes."

"But I can't either, Mom. See?" She'd folded over her belly and let her arms hang. Stupid joke. As the blood rushed to her head, she'd known all her dreams were ruined, even the modest ones. Not that she wouldn't finish high school. She always finished what she started; she was no quitter. But by the time she'd raised the kid and Andy, well, did they even let you into medical school past thirty?

As she walked down the middle of the gravel road, the pressure on her pelvis and legs increased. Only her boat-sized shoes prevented her from plowing into the packed earth. She lowered onto one knee to scratch her ankle where an invisible burr had worked its way into her sock and kept on walking and scratching, the wind eroding new hollows in her left ear. She passed the empty red truck.

She was halfway home when she finally sat and removed her burr sock. As she re-laced her shoe, an ache-pain-pressure-echo torqued through her body. Contractions had been sold to her by her mother as being, you know, kind of like menstrual cramps. She glimpsed something in the ditch. Beer box? Candy wrapper? When the pain echo subsided, she pushed herself up and crept down into the ditch, and then she saw it, deep in the swaying grass. The pink tulle that TV, neighbours, social media had been talking about for the last three days. The figure under the ragged tulle was curled up.

"Bettina?" Her kneecap glanced off a rock, but she kept her voice soft and placed her hand on tiny spine and ribs. "Bettina?" The girl's back was warm from the sun or life. She shook the thin shoulder and the girl made the sound of a kitten. "Oh god, thankyouthankyouthankyou. Up we go." She lifted Bettina, pinned her to her hip with one arm, and laboured up the ditch and onto the road. "When we get home we'll call your mommy and daddy, and they'll be so glad to see you. Are you thirsty? You must be thirsty. I'm sorry. I don't have any water. My mom will know what to do."

The creeping red truck surprised her. The driver leaned out the window and said, "Need a ride?" He slammed the truck into park and flung open the door. "Is that the girl?"

"Do you have some water?"

"Yes, get in." He herded them to the passenger-side door. "Step on the running board, and grab this here. My name's Duncan."

She plopped into the bucket seat with Bettina in her arms. Duncan looked about her dad's age, but bigger, dressed in camouflage windbreaker and pants. He got in, rolled up the window, and turned off the engine. The only sounds were Bettina's mewing and the wind outside. The truck rocked slightly, buffeted by the gusts.

Duncan took a bottle from the console and gave it to Natalie. The warm water created dark rivulets across Bettina's filthy face. She gagged and coughed.

"That's enough for now," said Duncan. "I have a power bar in here too."

"Let's just get her home. My mom will know what to do."

Bettina curled up around her belly.

"Do you or don't you want my help?" Duncan said to the driver-side window. "I've been tracking her over the last two days, you know. I figured she'd come out of the bush around here, and I was right. But you found her."

"I never thought we would," she whispered.

"Lucky. You just got lucky. I'm a big game hunter, you know. I can track anything: moose, deer, bears. I worked like fuck to get this good. What have you done? Lie on your back, looks like. But you found her." Duncan slammed his hands into the steering wheel. "You found the girl!"

"Her name's Bettina."

At the sound of her name, Bettina reached her scratched and bug-bitten arms around Natalie's neck and hid her face.

"I know what her fucking name is. It's fucking everywhere, isn't it?"

"Do you want the reward money?" She wasn't even sure there was reward money. She held Bettina tighter.

"I want her."

A second contraction twisted through her body.

"What the fuck? Are you having a baby right now?"

"My mom will know what to do." Natalie started crying. Big ugly sobs that filled the cab. "I didn't think she'd be alive. I can't believe I found her. And then I get into this truck. With you. And you're probably dangerous. Look at you. You're probably going to kill us, aren't you?"

"Hey, now. Don't talk like that." He shook his head violently, as if to dislodge something, and turned the key in the ignition, shifted into drive. "Sorry, I've got this anger thing, but I'm no murderer. And you're just a kid. Got to think positive or the bad stuff sets in, you know."

"I was so sure she was dead."

"Children are tougher than people think. Don't forget it."

The sun was low and the truck cast a long shadow that, though they drove slowly, seemed to race over the fields. Watching that shadow, she thought about time. How she was supposed to time her contractions. How she wouldn't turn it back even if she could. It seemed she was adapting. To the world of Duncan's truck and of lost little girls. Maybe she could adapt to anything. To the dream that was her future, with its rigid timeline, she could cycle in the unpredictable, the irrational, the frightening. Welcome these things until time became figurative and generous.

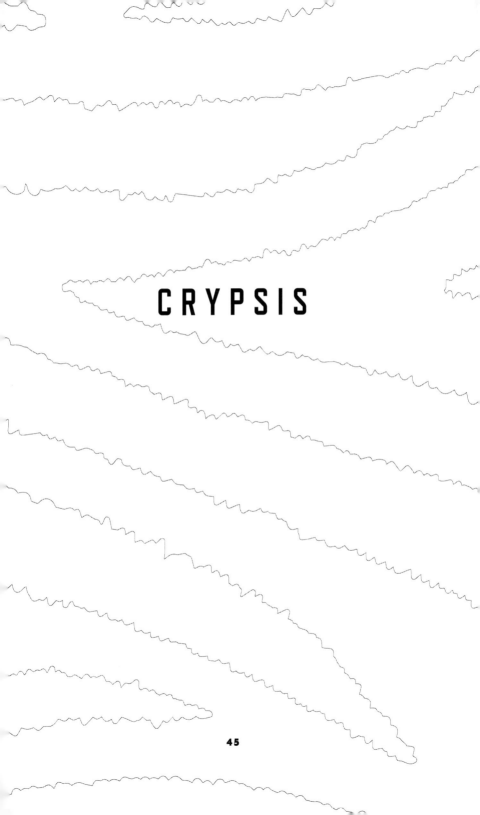

CRYPSIS

Lepus townsendii campanius @Hareofthefields · Sep 25
I'm a white-tailed jackrabbit, but my name in all its forms is misleading. In Latin it confines me to the fields, even though I've adapted well to your urban environment. In English I'm not a rabbit at all but a hare.

I'm on the phone with the library's marketing manager. She's called asking if I'd appear tomorrow on the morning show to promote the upcoming sexual health information fair, the catchy but unwise title of which is Sex in the Library. Does she know sex *is* had in the library — mainly, but at a guess not exclusively, in the public bathrooms — and is actively discouraged?

Over the low picture-book shelving from the second-storey windows, I see a smiling mother waiting to cross the street with two wholesome toddlers and a pile of book returns in a green wagon. They're on their way to Storytime. Nearby in City Hall square, a man with only a T-shirt against the spring chill is gesturing energetically and shouting at an elm. I'm used to such contrasting visions. Almost every glance through the library windows encompasses these two kinds of lives lived, reminding me daily how easy it is to slip from one to the other.

Take me, for instance. One day I discover a gorgeous hare mask in the programming supplies which I plan to use to tell an African folk tale to a class of grade twos. The next thing I know my only child, Eddy, is dead, and I'm wearing the mask full-time for reasons that are, though not exactly clear to me, clearly cracked.

The mask was made by fellow librarian Gabe, who has a background as a theatre artist, for the Br'er Rabbit stories he told before we all, again, became self-conscious about cultural appropriation. By the time I found the mask, we were back to telling a wide range of stories with renewed and mindful context, respect, or permission – having traumatized our young audiences with Nordic sagas and Germanic fairy tales for a few weeks – but the hare mask hadn't been dusted off yet. Gabe modelled the mask on the white-tailed jackrabbits that basically run this town and the likeness is striking. The eyes wide set, the ears long and black tipped, the colouring drab. This is no Easter Bunny, and with every telling, it helps me enter further into the story of Hare who was asked by Moon to bring immortality to humankind. Hare got the message wrong and instead brought mortality. Moon was displeased with Hare, and she beat him with a stick, splitting his nose, then assigned him the unpleasant job of shepherding the dead to the afterlife.

I identify with Hare as the bringer of death and feel I also deserve punishment for reading a cozy mystery while my six-year-old climbed a neighbour's two-storey aluminum ladder, fell, and died.

"**Sex in the Library** is getting so much media," the marketing manager tells me over the phone. "And then, Toba, with you and your bunny mask —"

"It's supposed to be a hare. The mask."

"Right. They asked for you specifically. The title was my idea, actually."

In my pre-mask days, I would have pointed out the potential pitfalls of a title like Sex in the Library or joked it up later with my co-workers, but they're keeping their distance – who can blame them? – and mixed messages are the least of my worries. I've never been on television before. I don't like the idea.

"Parents prefer to see children's librarians as sexless creatures." I'm making this up but it sounds true. "Am I the best candidate for the job?"

"Of course!" She tries flattery, describing how the social media posts featuring me and my hare mask inspire the most engagement. "We've doubled our followers since – What's wrong? How can we support you?"

I've heard this ominous phrase before, soon after I started wearing the mask full-time. HR introduced the topic of mandated therapy with, "How can we support you?" which felt more like, "How can we fire you?" At the time, my grief was liquid, the job and the mask barely containing it, but the counsellor recommended accommodation for my "avoidance mask made literal," and I wasn't fired. Instead, as the weeks went by, as with many Hare tales, things got tricksy, and I became small-city famous. Strangers greeted me on the street, shared sightings: "I stood behind her in line at Magic Java today. She stared at the puffed wheat squares the whole time but then only ordered a coffee." The local weekly profiled my style, identifying where I'd purchased each unremarkable item of clothing and accessory. Only the mask was remarkable. My kind husband, Mark, accepted all this and encouraged me to journal, like he was doing on the advice of his counsellor. It was helpful for him. He hadn't already experimented with dear diaries as I had — boys don't get diaries for their birthdays — and I'd found the practice horrifying. Leaking my thoughts, experiences, and feelings onto paper made them unreal, my words never capturing the whole of it and leaving only an embarrassing, banal slime trail. Sorry, Mark, no diary. But I felt compelled to share my new-found obsession with jackrabbits, so I started a Twitter account, @Hareofthefields, which gained over ten thousand followers. Now the library features my Storytimes on its YouTube channel and can't do without the mask.

And maybe I like the attention — who could say? I'm not sure what's behind the mask anymore. Maybe I've lost her forever, and my feeling right now is good riddance or, perhaps, who cares. I recognize the danger in this personal leave-taking, that it looks like a man yelling at a tree, but I tell the marketing manager, "I'll do it," and we discuss the key messages.

Lepus townsendii campanius @Hareofthefields · Jan 3
My young are called leverets. I hide them under foliage in a shallow depression in the ground. I leave them alone in their form except to bring food, but I have sense enough to stay close to watch for predators: hawks, foxes, coyotes, ladders.

After the phone call, I start my shift at the checkout desk. The rote, physical nature of the work feels good normally. I could do this in my sleep. Sometimes it seems like I do, but the phone call and the weird offer and acceptance of a television appearance has jarred me awake. I feel groggy and unbalanced. I check out a pile of picture books for a little boy who reminds me of Eddy – this happens sometimes – same hair swirl at the base of his skull. Without my mask, the boy's question would have rendered me instantly – a puddle of fat and bones and teeth and hair – but I answer, "I was an old mommy. I only had the one leveret."

The memories surrounding Eddy's death are these: shriek of aluminum ladder against metal eavestrough, a crash, spilled coffee, more shrieks – mine – grit-pitted knees, smell of wet leaves, siren's wail, Eddy's still-warm hand. But what I remember most clearly is the witness: a leggy jackrabbit, motionless against the spirea shrub, looking so like the artful mask I had just found. Long, black-tipped ears twitch. One bulbous hazel eye watches. Fur a mottled white-grey-beige, caught between its winter and summer coats. An interstitial space between seasons or between this world and the next. The animal observer seemed to hold purpose – guide, messenger, judge – seemed to mean something; something had to mean something.

"What?" The boy's mother is distracted by the baby strapped to her front.

"Your little guy just asked if I had kids of my own."

The mother doesn't ask any follow-up questions, frowns and soothes the baby as if she's fussing. Parents aren't wrong to be suspicious, what with the mask and their children's blind devotion. The moms and dads know me from Storytime and they sense I am a menace. Without the mask, I was. With it, I am library mascot, harmless eccentric, stranger to myself.

The boy places his chubby, trembling hands, palms down, on top of the books and looks up at me with terror and love. He wants a hand stamp.

"What do you say?" says his mother.

"Please."

"She can't hear you."

"Please."

Through the mask's eyeholes I peer into his soul. "You look like a dragon slayer to me." I press the dragon and knight stamps onto his soft hands and lean down to whisper, "You don't need to say please to me."

The knighted boy stares at his hands in awe. His mother stuffs the books into a diaper bag and pulls him after her. He watches me over his shoulder, one finger in his mouth, ignoring Gabe who has just finished running Storytime and is offering high-fives near the doorway. Left un-fived, Gabe looks hurt.

Lepus townsendii campanius @Hareofthefields · Mar 1
The expression "mad as a March hare" derives from our courtship ritual. We appear to go bananas during mating season. For males, spring hare fights involve rearing up on hind legs and punching, plus ear biting. While they sort it out, females wait around feeling superior.

I **excuse myself** from the checkout desk and end up in the sickroom off the staff toilets. It is within these walls, painted a Pepto-Bismol pink, that I pace, fidget, and storytell my way through another panic attack. It has become a habit, and I've got my recovery down to around five minutes. The pacing helps expend the nervous energy that would prove useful in the event of a mastodon stampede; the storytelling distracts.

To my imaginary and queasily pink Storytime audience I confess, "Once upon a time there was an old mommy. She met her kind man late, got married, and had a baby. By the time her son stopped toddling and started running, she was tired. She called her parenting style 'free range,' just like that, with finger quotes. You've got it, children. Try finger quotes with your parents tonight: put 'bedtime' in finger quotes and see how it goes. But even though the old mommy was tired, she truly believed in this method, remembering as she did running wild on the farm as a child, collecting frogs or grasshoppers by the handful and throwing them to the lucky chickens – free range themselves – to devour in a mania of white feathers. She wanted that feeling of blissful power and freedom for her son. Because, children, remember this: the feelings of power and freedom do not last. 'Neglectful' is the uncharitable interpretation of 'free range' and was the interpretation the old mommy's neighbours favoured as, from behind their front windows, they watched her son race up and down the sidewalk, leaving his bicycle on their front lawns, recreating the Juno Beach landing in chalk in front of their houses, and declining to send their own children – sad, pale prisoners – out to play. And those neighbours were right because one spring day, the old mommy's son, feeling blissful power and freedom, climbed a two-storey aluminum ladder, fell, and died."

Heart rate slows, trembling ceases. Nearly done.

I became a children's librarian because children possess qualities I admire, qualities rarely evident in adults: curiosity, creativity, honesty, capacity for wonder, wildness. They're another species. All done.

Lepus townsendii campanius @Hareofthefields · Mar 2
When approached by males during mating season, females leap straight up in the air and the courtship chase begins. Only if we're caught will we admit he'll do.

"Please don't go on TV tomorrow, Toba." This is Mark from the supper table. "Mom watches that show."

I wield an orange watering can. With the mask my peripheral vision is shot. To see Mark I have to square up. This directness tends to escalate arguments, which I regret.

"And eat something and stop watering. Succulents thrive in arid conditions."

The man is trying and I love him and he's suffering too. None of these facts permits me to stop watering my succulents or sit down for a proper meal or remove the mask. Kind Mark brought the plants home from the university after his department instituted a "take home your shit" rule aimed at one plant-hoarding mechanical engineer. Foisting a colleague's collection of succulents on me was as well-meaning as it was obtuse. Well-meaning: Toba needs a hobby to distract her from grief and hare obsession. Obtuse: succulents thrive on neglect and, since Eddy died on her watch, obviously Toba can handle that level of care. For a few reasons, I water the succulents multiple times a day.

"Arid means dry."

"Thank you, Professor."

"The signs of overwatering are all there." Continuing to apply reason to the problem, he reads from his phone and points. "Black spots, yellowing, translucent leaves, mushy –"

"Don't touch!" I slap his hand, and it bangs against the window ledge. More leaves fall. "Why don't you want your mother to see me on TV?"

"I've been telling her you're wearing the mask for the kids at the library, but this sex thing? It's too much."

I have to agree. It is too much, but now I feel as compelled to follow through as a jackrabbit in heat. I must act out madness, scream at an elm. That night, I suffer a version of my recurring dream. I'm crossing 25th Street on foot. I don't see the car turning left fast into my path. I hear an otherworldly shriek – metal on metal – which alerts me, and I pivot out of the way at the last second. The driver's side mirror clips my backpack. I spin, stumble off the street onto the lawn in front of an apartment building. Under a spirea shrub is Hare, the creature who emitted the horrible, metallic shriek. Horrible because Hare chose to save me, not Eddy. The dream draws the same conclusion every time.

Lepus townsendii campanius @Hareofthefields · 7h
Try and find me. Spring moult is done and my cryptic colouration makes me hard to spot. Crypsis methods include camouflage and nocturnality. Movement might give me away.

The next morning, I wait for my interview on a white vinyl couch. A spider struggles to climb out of a prop coffee mug on the low, tempered glass table in front of me. Across the studio, behind a giant's desk, a woman delivers the news of an earthquake. In the nearby floor monitor, the news reader's face is heavily made up and impassive as she reports the disastrous number of dead. I can't feel other people's sorrow either. Not truly.

Dave Blanc, host of the morning show, lounges on the other side of the couch, ignoring me and doing vocal exercises, "Potato, pumpkin, Pilates." It's like we're kids playing shipwreck on that white vinyl couch, Dave pretending to be a harmless, muttering castaway suffering from dehydration and sunstroke before he leaps up and shoves me off the lifeboat into the shark-rich waters. I know him from radio but here he is, the voice embodied, and it feels like a betrayal. I silently cheer on the spider who is now scuttling across the table. Then Dave sits up straight and sets a crushing sheaf of papers on top of it. His smile is too white. The camera operator counts three, two, one.

"Sex in the library!" Dave's voice booms. "It's not just a fantasy anymore. We have Toba 'Bunny' Burns with us from the public library to explain. What the heck is going on over there, Bunny?"

I adjust the mask, fitting it snugger, scramble to recall the key messages. "If your fantasy is to be a well-informed human being —"

"Sexy librarians. Is that it?"

The camera operator's shrug informs me this is Just Dave.

"It's a sexual health information fair. We've invited community agencies and experts —"

"Sexperts! Rabbits are known for their fecundity, right?"

"It's happening today from two to eight at the central library." I speak in a rush. Add something about our website and HIV testing. Despite Just Dave, I've communicated the key messages. Is my mother-in-law watching, sipping tea in her housecoat? Is she confused? She should be. I am. I don't know what I'm doing here, but I'm pretty sure I deserve it.

Just as I'm accepting this public humiliation as punishment, more punishment is delivered through a journalistic attack. "Tell me, Bunny, what's with the mask? Let's get to the bottom of this. What are you hiding?"

I wonder where Just Dave went. The questions make me go still as if a predator is nearby, circling, and I am camouflaged in my winter coat on the white vinyl couch, as if only movement will give me away. Humans are not built for hiding. Eddy's early attempts at hide-and-seek, squeezing his eyes shut behind a broom, were laughable. I glance at Hare in a floor monitor. Indeed, Dave. What's with the mask? What am I hiding? Where's the bottom? Good questions. These questions deserve to be asked. I deserve an interrogation. And yet nobody, for fear of who knows what answer, has asked. Not even that therapist who gave me a letter of accommodation. Regardless, this is the punishment I deserve. Other people have it worse or just as bad — I see them every day at the library — and they don't go around wearing hare masks, being accommodated, having their unremarkable styles celebrated, being trusted and adored by children, getting invited on television. And most of them haven't killed their children either.

"It's okay, Bunny. Take your time." Dave's tone has changed again. He leans forward.

Disarmed, I blurt, "Once upon a time there was an old mommy —"

The spider crawls out from under his sheaf of papers. It looks diminished, may have left a leg or two behind, but it's alive, prepared to carry on living in the public eye, though invisible to the viewing audience. I point but then think better of it and put my hand back in my lap. I don't want Dave to kill the spider.

And I do not resume my story, because it's a private confession, a story I tell myself and live inside. It's not up to Dave Blanc to forgive or to punish. To shove me off the lifeboat I've been wanting to jump out of myself. Neither is it up to the morning show viewers, kids in Storytime, @Hareofthefields' likers and retweeters, downtown office workers, marketing managers, theatre Gabe, kind Mark. It's certainly not up to a leggy jackrabbit.

I lift the mask off and cradle it in my lap. In the floor monitor I see a familiar, unremarkable face. There she is. Another middle-aged woman with private sorrows who works at the library. Humans *are* built for hiding, I was wrong. And without the mask, new sensations. I hear the whir of machine hydraulics and cooling fans, smell Dave's hair cream and the dirty mop used by the night cleaners. The recycled studio air on my skin is bracing; the light in my periphery blinding.

FAMILY STYLE

"**I know this** neighbourhood is trendy, but does it have to be so dirty?" said Colette. "Amanda *would* pick this restaurant just to make me uncomfortable."

Martin Woodrow stood arm in arm with his wife before a renovated brick warehouse. In the empty lot to one side, a faded realty sign from his company canted, heavy with snow. A cinder-block pawn shop squatted on the other lot, and across the street a group of men smoked in front of a homeless shelter. He conceded inwardly that Colette may have a point; their daughter *may* have intended to antagonize her mother with the choice of restaurant and, more acutely, with her fiancé, Bob, whom she has brought home to Calgary from Toronto for Easter weekend.

Endorsing Amanda's boyfriends had always been difficult — her first batch in adolescence included Nolan with eyeliner, Blaine on steroids, and Greg who didn't bathe — but Martin had always supported her choices. He was a good dad. And even though Amanda had taken "inappropriate boyfriend" to a whole new level, he was determined to welcome Bob into the family. Yes, Bob, his former colleague, who'd outsold Martin every year before being promoted to Toronto; Bob who'd flirted with Colette at every work barbecue; Bob who'd driven Amanda home from play dates with his own daughter, Brandi; Bob who'd run into Amanda on the street in Toronto last fall and thought something like, *Why, there's Amanda Woodrow, good ol' Martin Woodrow's daughter, Brandi's childhood friend. What's she doing in Toronto? A marketing*

executive already? My, my. Should I be avuncular? Not me.
I should ask her out on a date.

"The restaurant looks nice." Martin stated what felt like objective fact and favourable evidence of Amanda's intentions. The restaurant featured a retractable wall of windows behind which warmly lit young professionals of Calgary enjoyed a last supper before the sodium shock of family and Easter ham the next day.

"Like I'm not uncomfortable enough, having to see that man with Amanda. If he calls me Mom —" Colette tugged her arm free and shook her hand to send blood back to fingers. Was his grip that firm? "How was your run today? I had my best time yet."

"Good." He commented on Colette's run rather than answer her question, so not exactly a lie. Was his paunch that big? He hadn't gone for a run that day, having made an appointment with a client instead, and he never found running good. Running was good like Good Friday was good, the feeling more akin to crucifixion than resurrection, but he was, in theory, training to run a half-marathon in July. He knew he couldn't show up at the start line with stale-dated athleticism, but he'd worry about that later. First he had to get through tonight. He feared a scene.

"What was that?" said Colette.

The sound and feel of a snowball strike were imprinted from childhood, so he knew what had thudded between his shoulder blades. As to the motive, he could only guess. Why did anyone do anything? His broad, expensively clothed back might be irresistible to the man who was laughing at him from across the street. A tall, stringy man in a worn, red plaid jacket and unemployed work boots. Also, it was perfect snowball weather. Had to give him that.

"Just some guy having a little fun. Nothing to worry about."

But his throwing arm twitched in readiness for a snowball fight, reminding him of another Easter weekend just like this one when Amanda was a child. The family had gone snowshoeing in a park. At some point, Colette and Amanda had ganged up on him, discovering rare common ground. He'd let himself be tackled and took the pelting of half-formed snowballs and face washes happily enough but eventually reared up and out of this attack. To get his ya-yas out – because he wouldn't risk injuring his girls – he'd hurled a dense snowball towards an old elm, but he missed and hit the passenger-side door of a white Honda Civic. Though he couldn't be sure he'd made one particular dent in the battered Civic, he'd left his business card under the windshield wiper. "Wow, Daddy, you're strong," Amanda said, which was gratifying. Colette added with only an average amount of sarcasm, "That was a teachable moment." And he'd learned. Now was not the time to engage in a snowball fight with the underprivileged; ya-yas should stay on the inside.

A teenage hostess led Colette and Martin Woodrow through the cozy front lounge into a vast dining room where young, hip diners sat at close-set tables. They were escorted up an iron staircase to the mezzanine and seated in a corner from which they could survey the whole place, as had the long-gone warehouse bosses.

Colette said, "So this is where they put the geriatrics. Youngsters down below. Will you look at that one." She pointed at a woman with a neckline so gaping he could see all the way down the woman's shirt to her waist. Before he could look away, the woman caught him staring and offered a flirty finger wave.

"Do you know her?"

"No. How would I know her?"

"She waved at you, and I feel like I know her; I know she has an outie. And it seems young women have a thing for old real estate agents."

He shed his sports coat and rolled up his sleeves. "Remember, we're here to support Amanda."

"You support her, Martin. I, for one, cannot bless this union."

"Please don't start a fight tonight, Col." His wife claimed she expended all her emotional energy at work, but she generally didn't take shit from anyone. Amanda could use more of Colette's grit. Just enough grit to have rejected Bob. That level of grit.

A bearded waiter introduced himself as Cash and took their drink order: two barrel-aged cocktail specials, which sounded boozy enough to mute his anxiety.

"Cash is handsome," said Colette, "and is that *Rumours* playing? Maybe tonight won't be all bad. The food is supposed to be fantastic, and I plan to drink a lot. Plus, Bob'll offer to pay to show us how much money he's making. Amanda always was rather venal."

"Two barrel-aged Manhattans." Cash set their drinks down as Martin started fretting over the bill. "It's the best drink on our menu tonight. We get to try them all. That's why I'm always a little toasted at the beginning of my shift."

"Tell me, Cash," said Colette. "How much barrel aging does whisky need?"

Uh-oh, thought Martin.

"Um –"

"My wife's just teasing. Maybe you could call it a 'double-barrelled Manhattan'. Right, Col? Cash? What do you think?" He noted his pleading tone. Why couldn't he let a stranger's feelings get hurt? Who was this Cash to him anyway? Didn't he have bigger problems to worry about this evening?

"Dude. I'm totally passing that along to our mixologist."

Who was Cash? A fellow human, a kindred people pleaser, a more suitable fiancé for Amanda. These were only a few of the possibilities. Martin relaxed a little. He always did when he defended the little guy, even if it was against his own wife. That was just her way. He'd worry about the bill later.

"Mother, how're you doing?" In stressful situations, he reverted to his father's vernacular, but Colette didn't seem to notice. "Colette? Amanda isn't venal."

"Where's that Cash." Colette peered behind her. "Training makes me hungry."

"Remember Amanda's volunteer work at the food bank?"

"That was for school credit, Martin. Don't be naive."

"Cash, there you are." He knew he could enlist Cash to help soften Colette. "Could you bring us some bread? Champagne too? Also, keep Fleetwood Mac on repeat, would you?" But Colette's still-black, close-cropped hair flattened even closer to her scalp; the pale Irish skin she'd inherited from her mother was snowy. "What's wrong, Col. He's bringing bread."

"I was just thinking about that cow, Shannon. I'm not surprised Bob traded up. Remember when she kicked me out of her book club for being too confrontational? Can you believe it?"

He could believe it. "Nothing wrong with healthy debate."

"Exactly."

"She probably read too much into something you said. You know how she could let her imagination get away on her." He recalled standing over the barbecue, Shannon's cool hand on his hot burger-flipping arm, her warm breath in his ear murmuring, "We should keep an eye on our spouses, Martin. Or maybe," and she'd flicked her tongue over his ear lobe. He'd shut that nonsense down by shouting into the glowing briquettes, "No kidding! I like my burgers pink in the middle too!"

Cash brought bubbly and baguette. Bruxism had left Martin with a trick jaw so he avoided baguettes, but he marvelled at Colette muscling through the chewy bread. He often marvelled at her. When he thought of his marriage, he thought of this pine tree he'd seen while out on a hike one time. Its roots had grown around a sheared chunk of granite, embedding the rock. He supposed he was the tree in this metaphor, accommodating his angular, stubborn Colette. Or maybe he was the dull block of granite, the inanimate object improbably embraced by the vital life force. Either way, the marriage never wobbled. He set aside the vision he had of Bob in red mountain-man plaid with an axe over his shoulder. He wanted Amanda, his little squirrel, back scampering in the branches.

Why was it so hot? He loosened his tie. He swallowed the last of his cocktail and downed the champagne from his tiny coupe glass. The delicate object looked as if it could belong to a child's play set.

Cash materialized and refilled their coupes. "Are we waiting for the other guests, or should I bring the first course?

We call it 'family style' here at Taste — people serve themselves from shared dishes and all that, like families do."

"Bring it on, Cash," said Colette. "We're doing the full family tonight."

"Cool-cool. Devilled eggs coming right up."

Colette clapped her hands. "I haven't had devilled eggs since Mom died."

"I think we should talk before Amanda arrives."

"Talk about what? Devilled eggs?"

"No, our game plan."

"Mom's secret ingredient was pickle juice."

He swallowed his third glass of champagne and realized he should have eaten some baguette for ballast, because his vision swam when he saw his daughter and Bob together for the first time.

"Daddy!" Amanda stood on tiptoe to hug him. He looked over her head at Bob, whose face featured an impossibly relaxed smile.

"Martin." Bob gave his arm a surprise squeeze as he edged around the hug, not allowing time for a bicep flex.

Bob air-kissed Colette. She left a smear of lipstick on his cheek.

"Time to let go, Daddy."

"Sorry, honey." He released his daughter, talking through the throat pain that precedes tears. "I just miss you so much, my little squirrel. You're so beautiful. Just like your mother."

"Hi, Mom."

"Nice blouse, Amanda," Colette said.

Martin shook his head at her, but she continued on, heedless.

"Must be the neckline of the season."

"Bob bought it for me." Amanda touched Bob's hand and allowed him to push her chair under her.

The man was everywhere at once! And had bought Amanda that meagre thing she was wearing. Martin felt his teeth begin to grind.

"Calgary weather." Bob sat beside Colette, across from Amanda. "Shovels and snowsuits this Easter, eh?"

Martin forgot all small talk and lifted his soup spoon — now a microphone — announcing, "He is risen! He is risen, indeed!" He turned to Amanda, trusting she'd play along at their old game. "But wait, folks. He's turning around. Jesus is heading back into the cave. Unbelievable. He's rolling the stone back into place. Let's watch that replay. I think he's saying 'too cold.' Amanda, is that your read?"

Amanda took up her own spoon, "That's my read too, Martin. Yes, ladies and gentlemen: Jesus is too cold."

"Too cold to be our Lord and Saviour." He looked to Amanda for another comeback.

Bob picked up his own spoon. "But Easter Sunday is a day away, folks. He could turn this thing around yet."

Martin's spoon clattered onto his plate. *He* was Daddy, not Bob.

"Here come the devilled eggs!" said Colette.

He would have preferred any other man across the table from his daughter. Even that tall, homeless one who'd thrown the snowball. He could have helped him get his real estate licence, and, though smoking was a filthy habit, he could live with that. We all had our weaknesses. He began to worry about his capacity for welcome.

"Are you okay, Daddy?"

"He's fine." Colette nabbed a slithering devilled egg before the plate hit the table. "He's going for a high-water mark in the circumference of his armpit sweat. It's the extra weight he's carrying." She took a bite. "Is that caviar?"

"Looks like trout roe," said Bob.

"Don't be hard on Daddy. It's normal to put on a few pounds in old age."

"Bob hasn't, has he. Even though he, too, is old. Lean as ... Cash, have you tried these eggs?" said Colette. "Delicious! And we'll do the wine pairing."

"No wine for me, Cash, thanks." Bob turned to Colette. "It's the running. And the green smoothies."

"Bob isn't old." Amanda gathered up her long black hair, the static cling between hair and gossamer blouse throwing sparks. She scraped it all over to one side, but a few strands drifted over in Martin's direction. He'd see her back in Calgary yet. Maybe in a nice old two-storey down by the Bow.

"Yes, he is," said Colette. "Old, second-hand, even. And why don't you cut that hair? Watching you fuss with it makes me nuts ... Ooh, I love this song." The opening acoustic guitar in "Never Going Back Again" played.

"I like my hair long," said Amanda.

The theme of many fights between mother and daughter was hair, and he trusted Amanda grew her hair because she really did like it and not to prove something to Colette or — dear God — to please Bob. "We're running in the Calgary marathon this summer," he blurted.

"5 or 10 κ? I ran the Boston Marathon last year."

"We're doing the whole thing." Martin surprised himself

with this lie and searched for the facts of marathons in Colette's eyes, but they were closed in communion with Lindsey Buckingham. "The whole 20 к."

"42.2 к."

"That's what I said. 42.2 к."

"Oh, Daddy."

Colette sang along to the music, oblivious to his floundering.

Cash pried out the cork using a vintage corkscrew. Who needs a lever when you've got the arms of Cash? The arms Martin used to have. Cash poured wine for all but Bob while another server placed a steaming dish on the table. "Basque chorizo and gigante bean cassoulet topped with a soffritto of aromatics."

"Baked beans!" Colette heaped a pile onto her plate.

Was Amanda's sneer at her mother's enthusiasm? When he offered his daughter some beans, she made a face as if he were offering her a spoonful of baby shit. Would Amanda have a baby with Bob? Martin's gorge lurched. Would he even want grandchildren in that house by the Bow if their father was Bob, the man who was currently sorting through his small mound of beans, banishing bits of sausage, onion, and flavour to the cold, outer ring of his plate?

After a serving of beans scraped down Martin's throat, he set his fork down triumphantly. "Didn't your mother teach you to finish your plate, Bob? I remember being forced to stay at the table, gagging on every last cold pea."

"That must have been traumatic for you, Martin. Unhealthy attitudes towards food leave a legacy." Bob swirled his hands in front of his own flat abs. "I reject that approach and only eat what I need. Beans are full of protein and antioxidants —"

"You're full of beans." Truly, was that the best he could come up with? Where was Colette when you needed her?

Colette was singing along with Stevie Nicks now.

"Did you know," Bob said while Martin steeled himself to be schooled. "'The Chain' is the only song with a writing credit for all five band members? Fleetwood Mac was a cocaine-fuelled disaster when they made *Rumours*."

"Who's Fleetwood Mac?" said Amanda.

"Shaved broccoli salad with serrano ham, desiccated fruit, and heritage seeds, dressed with *sauce à la crème fraîche*." Martin read from the menu, which was typed onto a vintage library borrowing card, with a measure of awe.

"Mom's creamy broccoli salad!" said Colette.

"Will you stop that," said Amanda. "It's supposed to be ironic."

"The menu says they're 're-authenticating farmhouse classics,'" said Bob.

Martin drank and perspired.

And they ate: Colette humming, Amanda with delicacy, Martin with difficulty. Bob pressed his salad with a fork, squeezing out *sauce à la crème fraîche*, eating the sunflower seeds and bits of broccoli one at a time. With a teaspoon, Martin noted, like a toddler. Whereas he was a man. Or was he?

"Oh Daddy" played, and Christine McVie suggested he wasn't.

Saved-up worry over the bill made Martin's chewing and swallowing of *grass-fed beef brisket au jus on puréed rutabaga* — which Colette had translated as "pot roast and mashed turnips" — especially mechanical. Should he let Bob pay? Could he?

What did he owe? What was owing? Was he Daddy? Was he a man? With his last, flavourless mouthful of turnip, he remembered a bizarre icebreaker during some otherwise forgotten training session where he'd been required to state what kind of vegetable he would be if he were a vegetable. He'd chosen turnip because it sounded funny, but now he really felt like a turnip, boiled and mashed. He was the root of this mess: supporting, trusting, loving, peace making, welcoming, hosting dumb barbecues. Like a turnip would.

Turnip-hosted barbecues made him wonder out loud, "How's Shannon?" This got Colette's attention, which, he realized, he'd wanted. She appeared sated and was wiping her mouth with a cloth napkin when she froze at the mention of Shannon's name and shook her head curtly, warning him away from the topic. Since when was she the voice of reason? His mind scrambled for the particulars of Shannon. "Is she still doing equestrian?"

"Good memory, Martin. I memorize poetry to keep my brain shipshape. She took up riding again after the divorce. Stables a horse just outside Guelph. Loves it."

"Does she love you marrying Brandi's playmate?" These last words rose in pitch and volume to a throttled shout, and he knew he'd blown it. Knew he'd hurt his daughter. Knew Colette's warning had imagined this scene.

"Daddy!" "Martin!" They spoke with one voice.

"It's okay." Bob reached for Amanda's hand. "We should name our feelings. Get them out in the open." He nodded encouragingly to everyone at the table, especially to Martin whose cheeks were burning. "I'll go first. I love Amanda and I am not ashamed."

Bob had named a feeling – and an absence of feeling, Martin noted didactically – loudly enough that the woman with the outie was frowning up at him. *Bob's the creep!* he wanted to shout, but Amanda appeared flattered. Was she in some sort of Stockholm Syndrome situation? How had he not prevented this? Prepared her for the Bobs of the world?

"Wow, that felt great. Who's next?"

Colette sat straighter and fluffed her hair.

Finally, he thought, here comes the withering.

"No need to proclaim your love to all of Calgary, Bob. We get it. Love moves in mysterious ways, et cetera, et cetera. Amanda, I'm sure we'll come to accept your being together. We want to be supportive. Just understand that it may take us a while to get used to. Sound fair? Martin, will you calm down? You look like you're going to burst into flames. Now let's hear some poetry. Show us your great memory, Bob."

"'Shall I compare thee to a summer's day?'"

Where was his Colette? This one was conciliatory and encouraging poetry recitation. He suddenly remembered Colette flirting back at Bob while he, Martin, cooked burgers, confused about why most people preferred them well done. And here were Amanda, Colette, and Cash, plus some diners from a neighbouring table, gently applauding Bob's recitation. Even Cash, his kind of guy. Even Amanda, his favourite person in the world. Even Colette, his sheared granite or life force or whatever. But now he could not welcome Bob into the family. He could not stop Amanda and Colette from scrapping. He could not convince Amanda to move back to Calgary. He was not a good dad. His marriage metaphor was wobbly.

Everything wobbled as Cash brought dessert. "Strawberry cardamom *crème!*"

Martin picked up his spoon and announced, "Ladies and gentlemen, this looks like strawberry shortcake. Amanda, is that your read too?" She didn't pick up her spoon. "Cash, would you agree? Would you agree this dessert appears to be strawberry shortcake?"

"Yes."

"Why didn't you just say so, son?"

"I don't know."

"He doesn't know, folks. Back to you, Amanda."

Amanda stared at her dessert. Her cheeks two strawberries in whipped cream and white cake.

Martin placed his spoon beside his plate and stood up. He thought about naming a feeling: anger, yup, fear, you betcha. His dad used to say that all the time, *you betcha*. So corny, so embarrassing. Dads. He used to embarrass Amanda terribly when she was younger. The more he tried not to, the more embarrassing he became. He'd resurrected old concert T-shirts, the cotton stretching across his belly, and "re-authenticated" a pair of Converse sneakers. Why did he think that would work?

He'd done it all wrong; he needed a reset. Redo, they used to call it in the schoolyard. He could feel his ya-yas letting themselves out. "Family, I need some air. Too hot —"

He heard Colette call after him as he fled down the iron staircase. He barely restrained himself from sprinting past the woman with the outie, through the lounge, and out the front door. As it closed behind him, he inhaled a lungful of cool mountain air tasting of spring. Steam rose from his bare forearms. The sound of his blood's rhythmic surging supplanted stranger chatter, clacking dishes, fucking Fleetwood Mac. Physical relief riffled through all his senses. Across the street, a few men smoked, and the tall man with the red plaid jacket leaned up against the wall of the shelter. Martin reached down and sculpted a large dense snowball, his hot hands creating the perfect icy glaze, and lobbed it across the street. The snowball exploded on the sidewalk in front of the men and sent chunks of snow onto their jeans. Through the hail of retaliation snowballs, he ran stiff-legged towards them, an arm up to protect his face.

When he reached the men, he laughed and held up empty hands in surrender. He braced himself, hands on his knees, to catch his breath, brushed snow out of his hair. Ice water trickled down his hot cheeks, neck, chest. Glorious. But through the crisp air and second-hand smoke, and through the men's boyish, boastful replay – forgetting their problems for a moment – he smelled the muggy stink of restaurant food, every cooked ingredient compounded. Had he gazed at the restaurant facade only a couple hours ago and said, "Looks nice"? Who was that guy?

Redo.

He pointed at the restaurant and threw the first snowball. It slammed against the window with a satisfying bang. The rest of the men, maybe with less stifled anger, maybe with more uninhibited joy, followed his lead and began pelting the building. Behind the shivering glass, faces flinched and gaped while he scooped up wet snow, crafted snowballs from hell, threw ya-ya style.

YES
MIKE

"You should be department head," said Ashley. "Don't let Jason get it. Apply already."

Mike said he'd rather eat glass. He leaned against the kitchen counter in the break room sipping coffee they'd helped themselves to even though they didn't pay into Coffee Club. Jason organized Coffee Club, and everyone knew the department head position was his to lose.

"When you eat glass you bleed out of your ears." Ashley adjusted the scrunchy at the top of her head. "I saw it on *Oz*. Have you seen *Oz*?"

Mike had watched the whole series a few months ago during a television binge after Samantha moved out. He couldn't remember the glass scene amid the constant, vivid prison violence and grey anger of those weeks. He took a breath to ask Ashley which season.

"It's awesome. Anyway, being department head would be much less painful. I think." She jerked her head back to reposition her glasses. The lenses were the size of tea saucers. "Unless you ate glass while you were department head." She created a frame with her index fingers and thumbs and read the imaginary headline: "'Office Rival Grinds Glass, Serves in Co-worker's Chili.' You know how you like Tim Hortons' chili? But no one would do that to you, Mike. No way."

Then he remembered the scene in *Oz*: old gangster, blood seeping out of his ears and mouth, stumbling around a grim rec room, stunned and betrayed, metal chairs scraping and clanging onto the floor as other prisoners watch in horror or triumph or schadenfreude. "Do I need to watch my back, Ashley?"

"Please," she said, swatting away the question. "If anyone should be watching his back, it's Jason. Just kidding. I mean, everyone in Admissions hates him, even the students hate him. But not you! We just really think you have some good ideas, you're really great at your job, and you have nice hair. We all think so. Save us from Jason." She whisper-chanted: "Do it, do it, do it. Talk to Rollins. It's —"

Rollins' admin assistant, Janet, walked into the staff room, opened the fridge, and removed a jar of pork rinds.

"Hi Janet!" said Ashley. "Still on the Keto? I wish I had your willpower. I tried Keto once. Two hours in — I swear to you — I ate a Mars bar, even though I hate them, and a bag of Cheezies, which, okay, I love. Who doesn't?"

Janet backed out of the staff room. "It takes self-control."

"You bet, Janet. Thanks for the pep talk … Oh god, what is that smell?" Ashley whispered, "Was that Janet?"

The stench of sour milk squatted in the air and Mike pointed at the fridge. They grimaced at each other. Neither suggested cleaning it.

Mike returned to his cubicle, jangly with caffeine and picturing Ashley dressed in prison drab, then prison orange, sans scrunchy and glasses — scrunchy having been confiscated as a potential noose and glasses punched off her face by a fellow inmate on day one. She looked kind of sexy. Then he started to feel #MeTooIObjectify about the part where he's a prison guard with blue collar and billy club.

Maybe he should apply for the department head position. His gut said no. And his head too: the stipend was small, the increased workload significant, the respect gained minimal – they called the soon-to-be-retired incumbent Boss of the Staplers behind her back. But his gut and head always said no. That was his problem, according to Samantha, who'd described him as a No Person. When he asked what that was, she said, "The opposite of a Yes Person." Was Sam right? Was he a No Person? Did he have nice hair? Was he the only one who could displace the reviled Jason?

He spent the rest of the morning following up with the perennially stupid and hopeful prospective students. "I'm sorry you failed Physics and Calculus, but you kind of need them for Engineering. Have you considered the Humanities? I have an English degree." *And look where I am now.* Had Samantha meant he should be more ambitious? Shortly before she left, she'd asked where he saw himself in ten years. "With you," he'd answered with conviction, and when her head tipped to the left and her eyes narrowed, he added, "and our babies?" Wrong answer.

He began fantasizing about the fair and efficient meetings he'd run as department head. They would end on schedule while he maintained the tricky balance between telling people they were "heard" and telling them to cut out the useless chatter about "feelings." Action items would be acted upon and completed and meeting treats would always be home-baked – not by him, no, but by someone. Ashley? He would manage the department's social budget and office supplies with wisdom and creativity. He would be good at this, he decided. Uniquely suited to this opportunity. Yet humble.

After lunch, he strode into the administrative offices. A Yes Person. The open jar of pork rinds sat beside Janet's keyboard.

"Hi, Janet. Is Mr. Rollins free?"

She frowned at her computer screen and clicked her mouse many times, including several double-clicks. He caught a whiff of sour milk. Janet shook her head sadly and said, "Yes, he's between meetings right now. Just knock."

He was determined not to be psyched out by Janet, but worried when he realized he had no idea what Rollins did between meetings. Or during meetings, for that matter. Should he know? Before knocking, he paused before a glass-framed print of *Le Déjeuner sur l'herbe*. Was it appropriate in an office setting? He could see his reflection perfectly in the naked picnicker's pale flesh. He did have nice hair!

He knocked. Rollins called him in and gestured towards a chair across from his desk. The chair was set at preschool height, but he didn't want to adjust it, so he sat, resting his hands on his knees, chest level. "I'd like to be considered for the department head position, Mr. Rollins. What do I need to do?"

"Excellent, excellent." Rollins leaned back, spinning a mechanical pencil over his puffy knuckles. He too had a good head of hair, greying and longish. "I'm so glad you stepped forward, Mike. Most people don't want the responsibility, given the tiny stipend. I'm very pleased. Very."

"I have some ideas —"

"Of course Jason has thrown his hat into the ring as well." Rollins sat up straight and placed his elbows on the table, the pencil balanced and still.

"Of course."

"So I have a pretty big decision ahead of me."

"I could send you my —"

"No, no. I have everything I need to make a decision. I'll let you know tomorrow." The pencil took a final spin. "Hey, thanks again, bud." Rollins pushed his chair back. "Like I say, not everyone steps up like this. I'm really, really impressed. Really."

From his low chair, Mike rose on newborn calf legs. Rollins herded him to the door and shook his hand.

He slunk back to his cubicle.

Bud? Wasn't that what today's parents call their small boy children? *Good for you, bud! You went pee pee in the potty! Such a big boy. Yay!* He should never have let Ashley pressure him into this.

Shortly before lunch the next day, he noticed Rollins loitering at the threshold of his cubicle. Mike yanked out his earbuds and jumped to his feet. How long had the fucker been standing there?

"So this is your space," said Rollins. "I had to get directions. It's a maze up here on the second floor."

He waited with earbuds bunched in his fist.

"It was a very difficult decision, Mike," said Rollins taking a step backwards, "but Jason, he's aiming for administration, as you may know, and he really needs this, so."

Being the big boy that he was, Mike shook Rollins' hand for the second time in two days and thanked him. After Rollins left, he wiped his hand on his shirt and slumped into his chair. He lurked on Samantha's social media profiles for a while and sent a follow request to Jason. He swore under his breath as he untangled his earbuds and finally jammed them back into his ears. To a loud, semi-musical buzz, he composed an email whose greeting read, *Dear fuckfaces*. He saved it to his drafts folder and felt a little better.

"Hi?" Ashley poked her head around the cubicle partition. "I'm so sorry, Mike. Rollins asked me where you sat, and I kind of had to tell him. I thought it was worth a shot, you applying. I thought, maybe? Coming out for drinks later? Don't say no this time. Time for your medicine, mister."

It's true, he usually declined work drinks. Like a No Person might. He took a break from a student application for another social media update and saw that Jason had accepted his request. He studied Jason's profile for a few minutes then stood and looked in the direction of Jason's cubicle. A hand-drawn cardboard thermometer poked out over the partition wall, marking the progress in his latest fundraising effort. Refugees? United Way? The endangered hawksbill turtle? No matter. Based on Jason's social media activity, Mike knew he fucked the dog as much as anyone.

He met Ashley and a few others at the campus pub after work. They sat outside on the deck and justified their lives and actions to one another. He enjoyed his laid-back appearance in the reflection of Ashley's large prescription sunglasses. He didn't feel laid-back; he felt waves of heart-palpitating rage. This most recent rejection had stirred up rage over Samantha, and together the rages were producing something pretty unbearable. Good thing he could hide it all.

"I'm not a gossip or anything," said Ashley after her first pint of cider. "But did you know Jason is sleeping with some guy's wife? Yeah, I know." She nodded. "Who'd sleep with him? Apparently, my neighbour's cousin would. People just tell me stuff. I'm easy to talk to."

Mike nodded. He imagined Jason with pants around his ankles giving it from behind to some soccer mom with Samantha's face, his eyes steady on a cardboard thermometer labelled, *Satisfaction*.

After her second pint, Ashley had some advice, which she delivered loudly to the whole table. "You guys all know Mike applied for department head, right? And now he has no other choice but to kill Jason?" Ashley's third pint arrived and, in thanking the waitress with an air cheers, sloshed cider onto her dress. "He's so transparent, that guy. All the community engagement. All the staying late and coming in early. He's a pointless go-getter who has no other goal on this planet but to become the boss of people who do stuff. Therefore, he should die."

Mike got into it eventually. Drinking helped stifle the unhealthy combination of angers, and he joined in with the laughing, riffing, carrying-on.

Brooding and regret came later. Enough brooding and regret over the weekend to get him to work early Monday morning. Jason might have the right idea. Obviously, the guy had some sort of weird charisma, not only career-wise but also in his private life. Jason was so alluring that a woman – who still bore a striking resemblance to Samantha in Mike's imagination – was risking her marriage for him. So the question was, *What would Jason do in Mike's place?* And the answer: act like the perfect employee. A Yes Person thing to do. Look good and be good at your job. Because soon Jason would be promoted out of Admissions, and Mike's colleagues would hoist him on their shoulders and shout, *Huzzah!* He would wield his authority lightly but judiciously – and then a few months down the road, who knew? His gut might start saying yes. And Samantha might come home.

He processed three sets of incomplete applications while it was still quiet in the office and was congratulating himself on stowing his earbuds and phone in his top desk drawer when he heard the sound of running. After a carpet-muffled thudding, Ashley lurched into his cubicle. "I didn't mean it," she hissed, glancing over both shoulders. "I wasn't serious. I always do this, I'm joking and people take me seriously, like I don't sell it properly or my timing is off. They say it's all about timing. I blame my father. He only had one expression."

"Get to the point, Ashley. I'm working."

"I didn't mean you should really kill him," she whispered. "Murder is wrong you know."

"What?"

"How can you be at work today? Here they come!"

She should probably cut down on her drinking. He'd set her a good example next time. Yes People did not allow themselves to become distracted. But then came the purposeful strides of large men with squeaking utility belts. "Are you Michael Benson?"

No Mike really wanted to say no, but Yes Mike nodded.

"Come with us."

"What's this about? What happened?"

"You can help us with our inquiries."

Mike was co-operative. He led them through the maze.

Ashley's scrunchy bun peeked out over her cubicle partition, and light glinted off her lenses. He winked, reassuringly he thought, but she bleated and ducked down. Within minutes, they'd descended in the elevator and were out the heavy glass doors and into an idling police car.

He found himself in a small room, not much bigger than his cubicle, where he was made to wait for a bladder-splitting length of time. They let him out to pee and led him to another airless, grey room. Two men, two chairs, a garbage can, and a tablet on a table. The man in the suit directed him to sit down. "I'm Detective Morin and this is Detective Schmidt."

The younger man, in shirt sleeves and loosened tie, slouched half-on, half-off the corner of the metal table.

"Thank you for your co-operation, Michael," said Morin. "Do you know why you're here?"

Even Yes Mike couldn't answer yes to this question, but Morin didn't seem to be listening for an answer. Instead, the detective pointed his chin at Schmidt and then towards the door.

Schmidt whined, "Why do I always have to get the coffee?" To Mike he said, "We got shitty coffee. And water, I guess. Want some?"

"Water, yes. No! Coffee, please."

The heavy metal door slammed behind Schmidt.

"Fucking guy," said Morin. "Do you work with any shit-heels, Michael? I do. You know what gets me, though? More than his shitty attitude? The guy – listen to this – the guy, no matter the shirt, always has a stain in the exact same spot. How does he do it? One day it's tomato sauce; the next it's egg yolk. You just never know. And yet you know — that's the thing. One day he'll show up with a smear of toothpaste spit on there, and I'll lose it. I just hope I don't do anything drastic, like you."

Schmidt returned scowling, fresh chest-level coffee stain on shirt, and handed over a Styrofoam cup that slipped through Mike's sweaty palms and plopped onto the desk.

"We need to ask you a few questions." Morin fingered the tablet and pointed at the glowing screen. "Mike, this is why we're here."

The screen showed a man lying face down on blood-soaked carpet surrounded by broken glass. Jason's pelt of brown hair an immobile Lego accessory even in death.

Mike pivoted off his metal chair and onto his knees, vomiting into the garbage can. "Sorry," he said, his voice echoing in the can.

"Nervous, bud?" said Morin.

"Now you're sorry," said Schmidt. "Sit up, Mike."

The detectives seemed to get along just fine after that and asked the same questions over and over, just like the police procedurals he'd consumed during the breakup binge: anxiety, boredom, painful self-examination, plastic-wrapped sandwiches, crying. What were these publicly uttered threats (pub), the fuckface email (drafts folder), and could his motive be jealousy over Jason's promotion? Schmidt asked about his relationship with Ashley, and Mike said he hadn't thought about it before. "We're friends, I guess."

Finally, Morin took a call on his cell, and Mike felt the familiar barometric pressure change that signalled the end of a work day. "Cut him loose?"

Schmidt smiled. "It's your lucky day, bud."

By any measure, day-long police detention was not a good start to becoming Yes Mike. As soon as he got home, he went to bed and stayed there, only getting up to drink water, eat cereal, and use the bathroom. He measured time by the number of pails he dumped from under the toilet's cracked water tank. When he reached ten-pail sleep territory, he decided it was probably time to check his phone. Over another bowl of cereal and, despite all the sleep, unrested, he read his texts. Several were from Ashley.

Are you okay

How are you doing

Hello??????

I'm sorry!! Take your time

I made you a lasagna and left it with your building manager

He looked hungry

Did you get it

OMG the husband was charged with Jason's murder!!!!!!!!

Guess he was the jealous type

Who isn't

Call me!!!!

She even left a voice message. "We miss you, Mike. Don't we, guys!" Some shuffling, a pause, and a nasal voice saying, "Come on [muffled something or other] such a creep." Then back to Ashley with a chirpy, "Call me!"

That's when he felt the body-sagging relief of a near miss: the dusty *whoosh* of a city bus as you're about to step off the curb; catching the autocorrected "fuck" for "fun" before hitting send on a text to your mother; being eliminated from a murder inquiry. But did his colleagues think he was a creep? Did they believe he'd done it? Would Samantha think No Mike was capable of murder too?

He was still hungry. He found some iffy shaved ham in the fridge and wrapped it around a dill pickle. Something about the ham-pickle reminded him of his grade five classroom with its persistent smell of chalk and cold cuts. Mr. Prosko had seated Evan Blanchard beside him in the doomed hope he'd be a good influence on Evan, but Evan was much too powerful, pestering him day after day, and finally goading him into throwing an eraser at Mr. Prosko's head. That eraser left his hand with the force and accuracy of the powerless, but even in his windup, with tears of frustration and regret and fear in his eyes, he'd known Evan would be blamed.

With that memory, Mike's feeling of relief pivoted or maybe warped into the feeling of just having gotten away with something. The feeling of having cleverly evaded justice. With enough pressure, he was capable of anything. It *could* have been him. He could imagine what might lead someone to put ground glass into an enemy's chili. What might cause a cuckold to smash a rival's head into a patio door. Most people denied their potential for monstrousness, but not Mike, not now. To the idea of monstrousness, he said yes.

When he returned to work the next day, he did so with the swagger of a badass, a person of interest, a prison inmate, a man with a billy club, the last man standing. Strutting through the office, he smiled and nodded to right and left at his co-workers, many of whom avoided eye contact or made smile shapes with their lips. Just as he thought. He paused at the makeshift memorial in Jason's cubicle where someone had rigged up a new cardboard thermometer which tracked donations to Jason's "in lieu of flowers" charity, a shelter for women fleeing domestic violence. Despite the obituary's instructions, the cubicle overflowed with flowers and teddy bears. Why teddy bears? Weren't those for dead children? He patted his pockets, reflexively, to see if he had anything to contribute to the pile of gifts. He found a pen and placed it in the lap of a bear dressed like a dandy in cravat and blazer. He continued to his desk and logged on to his computer where he read an email from HR outlining how hugs were encouraged "due to grief." The memo also included a link to their sexual harassment policy. He snorted.

He turned from his screen at the sound of tapping on the flimsy trim of his partition wall. Ashley's hair hung down in glossy, styled curls, and her glasses were gone. Her cheeks were shiny spots of colour, and her arms were straight at her sides ending in tiny fists. She jerked her head back to reposition phantom glasses. "Mike, I have something to say to you. Here it is. I never, ever believed you killed Jason. I'm your friend. I would never. Also – no, please, Mike, please let me finish." He hadn't made a motion to interrupt her. "Also, I'm sure you already know this already, but I need to make it clear to you that I said nothing – nothing! – to the police about that bananas conversation we had at the pub. Note to self: Self, one pint is plenty. I'm no snitch." She scratched her neck where patches of red bloomed.

"Ashley." Mike stood and drew her into their first ever hug, an HR-sanctioned hug. She breathed wetly on his neck.

He spoke into her coconut-scented hair. "I know you'd never do anything to hurt me." The hug tightened. "And I have a feeling Rollins is going to give me that job. Should I apply?"

The humid patch on his neck cooled as Ashley held her breath and Mike, the future leader, mindful of policy, released her to let her talk.

ENFORCER

I **pressured Ty** into coming to the fall dance with me. I told myself I was helping him, but I probably just wanted a night out – let Brad put the kids to bed for once, was how I was feeling. After a shift at the care home, especially when Dad had a bad day, I could barely crank open a can of soup and slop the contents into a pot. Sometimes you get tired of taking care of people. *Grow up!* you want to shout to the world. *Don't be so helpless!* To which the fair response from the world would be, *Do I know you?*

Ty's my twin brother who at thirty-six was living in my basement, working as a handyman at one of our town's two motels, and in season playing senior hockey. The dance was a team fundraiser, but Ty wanted to stay home and study. He was turning over a new leaf, he told me, and had even quit drinking. He'd started another online course – hotelier school this time – but I wasn't counting on any virtual graduation ceremony. With one muddy boot of my reasoning in Ty's past failures and the other in some Lifetime Christmas movie, I thought he needed a girlfriend, not an education, and I told him he should get himself out there. Maybe he'd meet someone at the dance. "Some girls like a guy with broken teeth and hands that won't close anymore, makes them feel safe." I could say stuff like that to him.

As a result, the night of the dance Ty came upstairs with a blue necktie hanging loose around his collar and pants puddling around his cowboy boots. I already had on my jeans with the bejewelled pockets keeping every wobble in

95

place and my hair and makeup set to Barbie. I smelled like accelerant.

"Abby, what do I do with this thing?" He pulled at both ends of the tie.

"YouTube."

Our mother had neglected to teach us many basic life skills before leaving for a leathery Floridian who sold scrap scavenged from the ocean, but together we figured it out, and, though Ty couldn't get the top button done up around his thick neck, the look was as good as it was going to get. As I kneeled, stapling his pant hems, I asked who'd tied his ties when he was playing hockey in Brandon.

"Kelly." His tone suggested only a stranger would ask. "Well, he tied it once and I kept it done up."

"Kelly? The genius who quit a professional hockey career in Germany to move back here?" Except for the abandoning-your-family part, Mom had the right idea.

Ty said there was no point giving Kelly a hard time. Wasn't there? Let me recap. At fifteen, Tyler Dahl and Kelly Morrow were both drafted by the Wheat Kings — Kelly in the first round; Ty in the eighth. While Kelly went on to Europe, Ty was cut after breaking the coach's nose. I'd heard all about the coach and maybe said something to Ty about the guy needing a punch in the face. Dad received Ty's return from Brandon like he had Mom's departure to Florida: without comment. And I resented Kelly, because if I didn't, who would? It should have been Ty in Germany. Who doesn't need an enforcer?

Was I hard on people? People who deserved it, sure. Exhibit: Mom. She'd invited us to stay on her boat over Christmas, wanted to meet Brad and the kids. Ty thought we should consider it, while my thinking on the question started and ended with, "Fuck that." Ty didn't push it. He was loyal like that, and I loved him. He was a part of me. All those months we spent floating in amniotic fluid, becoming uncomfortably entwined, never being apart when we were little. I even thought we were the same person for a while. Dad told me about a time when we were two, and he was shopping at the Co-op. We were trapped in the grocery cart, and some woman asked my name and I said, "Tyandabby." When she asked Ty his name, I answered for him. "Tyandabby." Wasn't it obvious?

When it was time to leave for the dance, the whole family assembled in the entryway for what I hoped would be a brisk and tearless goodbye. Brad wrecked it by telling Ty he looked like a goof without a belt. Holding Anson in one arm with Marie clinging to his leg, Brad unbuckled and whipped off his own belt to give to Ty, but he elbowed Marie and set her to wail in the process. That got Anson going. The belt had been a birthday present Marie helped me pick out, and the buckle was too cowboy large and shiny, but now I regretted not having bought Ty one as well. We were all rattled by the goodbye, but Ty and I finally escaped into a gusting September wind. My shellacked hairstyle split and flattened, and my brother's tie blew up to vertical above his head as if it would lift him off his feet by the neck and hang him.

The town hall was decorated with Christmas lights and smelled of the buns and cold cuts brought in for midnight lunch. Stage lights and kitchen lights shone at either end of the hall, and the senior hockey team ran the bar from the kitchen. A country cover band was playing the first set and the old-timers were having their turn. They danced beautifully, but I knew I'd be giving some of them sponge baths soon enough.

"I like your belt, Ty," said Felicia as she stamped his wrist at the admission table. Felicia, pale as icing sugar, worked at the bakery.

Ty looked down at his waist and pointed a thumb in my direction. "Not mine."

I bought too many drink tickets from Felicia, still unused to Ty not drinking and distracted by all the attention over his new look. In the parking lot some pre-loader had shouted from his tailgate, presumably about the tie, "Where's the funeral?" To which I replied, "I'll send you to yours, dillweed!" Dillweed remains my favourite insult; it's old-fashioned, incomprehensible, and can be applied to young and old alike. I've cleaned up my language a bit since having the kids. I guess my point is, no one lets anybody change around here without an insult or a fight.

Ty headed to the kitchen for the bar shift he'd inherited from a lazy defenceman. My plan was to hang out with him and be the girlfriend spotter — I'd already ruled out Felicia — but before I could join him, I was forced to chat with Ruth, who smelled like scented maxi-pads, and Terri, who'd dated Ty in high school until she got knocked up by Stink. I mean, really, the guy's nickname was, and still is, Stink. Ruth and Terri were non-starters. Then I saw Dr. Ahmed.

"Lovely Abby," she said, reaching for my hand. "How is your family?"

I'm always nervous around sophisticated people, so I rambled about how Marie had started referring to herself in the third person and Anson's favourite dinosaur was the brontosaurus, not the T-Rex, which made Brad think he was going to grow up gay or vegan. Which didn't make me look very sophisticated at all, but domestic overshare was also blocking to avoid talking about Dad. She always asked about him, and I almost couldn't talk about him without crying. Dr. Ahmed had arrived in town before we'd moved Dad to Aspen Grove, where I work in the city. He was only uncharacteristically talkative at that time – that was when he told me the Tyandabby story – when he'd only just realized nothing in life made any sense.

Me, I've always known life doesn't make sense, so a question bubbled up in my murky puddle of a brain: would a medical doctor date my brother? Dr. Ahmed was beautiful and she was loving and non-judgmental. She'd delivered Marie after a forty-two-hour labour, and she still called me Lovely Abby. I didn't know how Ty would do with Syrian food, but then he was only too happy to eat whatever I scraped off a baking sheet. He'd eat whatever was put in front of him. Or maybe he'd learn to cook. Anything was possible.

"Have you met my brother, Tyler?" I pulled her by the hand to the kitchen where Ty stood behind the counter with tie tucked between shirt buttons, belt buckle glinting, palms forced flat on the countertop. He'd already set up tidy rows of opaque plastic cups with measures of liquor in them, ready to be handed off quickly for a rush on booze. They reminded me of the cups we used to apportion pills to our residents.

They'd met. Of course they'd met. Enforcing the unwritten rules of hockey meant injuries, and she could have treated him for, take your pick: lacerations, dislocations, concussions. No, not concussions, he just slept those off. On game nights, even during bedtime stories, my own knuckles throbbed.

But the kids knew the truth about their uncle, knew that when he wasn't enforcing unwritten rules, he was gentle and kind. What other man in town would let Marie paint his toenails?

"Mix is over there, Dr. Ahmed." Ty pointed to the adjacent wall where a plywood table sagged under a dozen two-litre bottles of Co-op brand pop.

Look at the woman! I wanted to shout. *Does she look like she wants off-brand pop?* "Would you like some wine instead?" I asked, helpful like always. "It's from a box and it makes your jaw ache but only on the first few sips."

"Thank you, no. I do not drink alcohol."

"Many Muslims don't drink, Abby," said Ty gently.

I was embarrassed but also surprised Ty was taking those hotelier classes seriously. Dr. Ahmed rubbed my shoulder, somehow conveying sympathy while looking over it – a doctor's trick? – and I saw her face become even more beautiful. I turned to see who she was smiling at, and any hope I had for Ty's chances with her evaporated, because it was Kelly Morrow. The man could be a movie star, I'm telling you. Tall, sandy hair, sleek European clothes, face unscarred despite years playing serious hockey. I glanced at my stocky brother, his keloid scars set into relief by dark stubble. Not even fair.

Kelly said, "Hey, doc," to Dr. Ahmed – gross – and kissed her on the lips – yuck.

I heard the tock of a plastic cup on the counter behind me and turned away from this exotic display of public affection to take a big gulp of wine. I felt rejected. My jaw ached. I watched Ty's face split into a goofy-toothed smile when he, too, saw who it was. Why did he love that guy so much? Not only had Kelly taken his spot in Germany and stolen the best woman in town, but he was also George Morrow's son and – eye roll – heir to the Morrow Motel empire. George was Ty's boss at the motel, and it was Ty over the past several months who'd made the motel less than disgusting: replaced carpets, scraped the crust of ketchup chips-and-beer barf off the bathroom tiles, planted annuals in the weed-infested window boxes. Where was Kelly? Wearing tight pants in Germany, that's where.

"Row," shouted Ty in his rink voice. "Give it a rest."

Kelly strode into the kitchen, held Ty's face roughly, and growled, "Brother, you look like shit." Which was their love language, I guess. He lifted Ty into a bear hug. "Set us up."

Ty grabbed two vodkas from his pre-poured rows, and they drank them in one go, which could have explained the desperate blinking, but I didn't think so. Just cry already, babies.

Kelly pointed at Dr. Ahmed. "I'm taking that one out two-stepping." I was like, have some respect, she's a medical doctor, but he brushed my elbow on his way to her, spilling some of my wine. "You should take better care of that brother of yours, Abby. He's a beauty."

"You made me spill." Of course I was taking care of Ty. Who said I wasn't? "Dillweed."

Kelly winked at me – winked! – and caught Dr. Ahmed around the waist. He gave her a quick two-step tutorial, then spun her in among the old folks. She appeared to love two-stepping, and they danced beautifully together.

A ruckus drew my attention to the entrance where George Morrow had skipped a step, striding past the admission table, entitled as a tomcat, as Felicia pleaded, "Excuse me, George. Excuse me."

My brother was watching too.

I asked him, "What's with Europants and Dr. Ahmed? How did I not know they were a thing?"

"Yeah, she's why he's back."

"You tell me everything," I said, altering reality to conform to my understanding of all things Tyandabby. I considered, not for the first time, the possible universe of things Ty wasn't telling me.

George snuck up beside me on his stupid tomcat feet and said, gazing towards the dance floor, "Showboat, that one. Always his problem."

I was inclined to agree with this assessment of Kelly, but that would be agreeing with George Morrow. "George, a ray of sunshine as always."

"Same sass as that mother of yours. Spitting image too."

"What'll it be, Mr. Morrow?" said Ty before I could ratchet up the sass. Mom had left when she was around my age, a fact I hadn't considered before.

"Rye." George didn't produce a drink ticket.

"Kelly's not a showboat." Ty handed George a cup from his tidy, pre-poured row. "He's just better than everyone else."

"Guess what he told me," said George, not inviting any guesses. "Told me he's not playing senior hockey."

Ty looked genuinely confused, like that time Dad threw a birthday party for Mom shortly before she left us, and she emerged from her stuffy bedroom in a dress and makeup, smelling of perfume and said, "Come to Mommy for a hug, darlings." We didn't see her outside her bedroom much in those days, and she rarely hugged. Rule changes have always thrown Ty off his game.

"Thinks he's going to make over the motel," George continued. "Rebrand, he calls it, boutique or some shit."

"He'll be great at marketing. I'm not so good at that." Ty shrugged, the muscles around his neck bunching up like a pit bull's, and I knew he'd never be the face of hospitality no matter how hard he studied. Not even fair. His failures were my failures.

George muttered something about "the Twitter" and moved towards the mix table.

"What a dick. I look nothing like Mom."

Ty swallowed another shot.

"I thought you'd quit," I said, though I was secretly pleased. I hated drinking alone.

"You're so fucking hard on people, and you're not helping. He's my boss, Abby. Jesus."

This anger felt like it came out of nowhere. Whose side was he on? I remembered a Pictionary game where Ty had drawn a horizontal line, and I guessed "ocean" immediately and correctly. The other players moaned about "twin power," but I knew Ty was drawing the ocean: not a table, not a road, but the ocean, with its terrifying depths, strange creatures, and scrap metal. After that, he never wanted to play on the same team. He said it wasn't fair; I said, "Yes, exactly." It hurt that he didn't want to be Tyandabby, hurt like a dislocation, but I'd forced the ball back in its socket, over and over.

I handed him the rest of my drink tickets in full sulk. "This should cover your drinks, and, hey, why not the Morrows' too?"

"Sorry, Abs. I just need you to —"

Dr. Ahmed and Kelly reappeared flushed and gorgeous. Kelly excused himself from her like some sort of gentleman to go catch up with Ty. That left Dr. Ahmed and me. Still sulky, still avoiding talk about Dad, I asked about her and Kelly since Ty wasn't sharing. Apparently, they'd met the previous summer at the farmers' market over a basket of kohlrabi. Kelly had said, "What are those things?" and she'd said, "The hearts of monsters." It was all a little too meet-cute until I learned they were getting married despite neither father's approval. I imagined a Syrian version of George.

And, I mean, what can I tell you about George Morrow? Let's start with the ABC's: asshole, blowhard, cretin. I don't know how Kelly did it, growing up with that man, but whenever I see George, I'm reminded of when he and I were of one mind. He was coaching the bantam team, and Ty and Kelly were wingers on the same line – Ty providing the assists and the protection; Kelly finding the net. The brawl started when my ex-boyfriend, Shane, who'd cheated on me with some skank from his town, high-sticked Kelly and I thought, here's my chance. While Ty threw down his gloves and started punching Shane's helmet, George screamed at him from the bench to "fucking kill that fucker!" I couldn't have agreed more. As Kelly waltzed in listless circles with the star from the other team, Dad left in disgust, and I stood with two flat, cold palms slapping the Plexiglass, hoping Ty wouldn't get hurt but proud of him too and wishing I could help somehow, but, really, I knew he'd be fine and I was helping. I could feel Ty like an extra limb, the one I used for punching and kicking.

I recalled my *kill that fucker* instinct as I watched Kelly resting on his elbows, leaning over the counter close to Ty. Did my brother feel as uncomfortable as I did sharing common ground with George Morrow? Or maybe it was different for an enforcer, being the actual arm of violence rather than the endorser, sick bystander, fan, coach, sister instigator. I couldn't hear what Ty and Kelly were talking about, but they glanced at George by the mix table. He was on everyone's minds. I mouthed "kohlrabi?" to Ty and rolled my eyes – George didn't deserve this much mental space – and Ty's broken-toothed smile gave me courage. He was still on my side. We were still a team.

"**I need another** drink," George bellowed, approaching the bar. "My-oh-my, a tie on Ty."

When he sensed people enjoying themselves, did he made it his mission to ruin the fun?

"Rye's on me, Mr. Morrow."

"On me," I corrected. This Dr. Seuss needed more than a drink.

"And twinkle toes over here. Too scared to play hockey back home. Dahl, you'll protect him, won't you?"

"Always has," said Kelly. "Hey, Abby, remember what your brother did to that kid who was always calling you Little Orphan Abby after your mom left?"

I laughed with Kelly at another *kill that fucker* memory. "Rink-rat skull, meet metal bleacher."

"I didn't mean to hurt him that bad," mumbled Ty.

"You didn't, not really," said Kelly. "He was in resource way before that."

I covered my mouth, copying the muffled buzz of our elementary school secretary over the intercom: "Timothy Barton (squawk) please report to the resource teacher in the library (squawk). Bring your pencil case this time, Timothy (squawk)."

Kelly and I laughed; Ty didn't; Dr. Ahmed appeared confused by the insensitivity of it all.

And George, ignored for a few minutes, looked furious. He jerked his chin towards Dr. Ahmed. "It's this one, isn't it? She wants you to quit."

Kelly turned away from his father, said, "That's enough," and put an arm around her.

Dr. Ahmed's forehead wrinkled.

Those same wrinkles had appeared around my thirtieth hour of labour with Marie. Dr. Ahmed did not deserve this, and have some fucking respect, was my feeling. And Ty thought Kelly, who was just trying to change, was someone worth protecting, so I did too. We were loyal that way. I had his broken-toothed courage, my mother's sass. I was hard on people.

My vision narrowed and I felt light-headed, anger only ever needing the lightest of breaths to flare up. I had not cowered in a corner or cried quietly under Timothy's bullying. I'd found his weaknesses and enumerated them with Ty at my back. Always with Ty. And now Ty had gone from flat palms on the countertop to curled hands in the mould of hockey gloves, so I did the same for George, a seasoned bully, as I had for Timothy. I enumerated George's weaknesses as I saw them, quickly touching on each of the ABC's.

George said, "Shut your sister up."

Ty reached over the counter, grabbed my jean jacket, and hauled me behind Kelly, pinning me to the counter, while I craned around, still talking because Ty couldn't shut me up, just protect.

After my speech, I was elated for a moment. My vision widened and I felt whole. Life didn't make sense, but sometimes you force a little sense into it, give it some rules. I looked to Ty, sure he could feel what I was feeling, but I did not see elation. I read his face as clearly as I'd read the ocean from a horizontal line. Ty's face said, *Do I know you?* and I saw that I wasn't taking care of him, I wasn't helping. Instead, I'd cost him another job and shoved him into a fight. A fight that wasn't even ours. Had I shoved him into every fight he'd ever been in? Had I sicced him on the bullies, mistake makers, bigots, cheaters, the other team, since the beginning?

"Bitch." George was still there – why? – and my words had changed nothing for him. "Just like your mother."

Despite the mucky, dragging feeling of having failed my brother, failed Tyandabby – *Do I know you?* – I remained hard. I thought *kill that fucker*, and in my imagination Ty didn't stand behind the bar conciliatory and apologetic. Didn't stand there with curled hands in the mould of hockey gloves. Instead, he vaulted over the counter, scattering tidy rows of plastic cups with single shots of vodka, rye, and rum, and mid-leap ripped off his belt, swinging it with all the momentum he'd gained in the jump, so that the heavy buckle sliced through the air, reflecting the twinkling Christmas lights in its arc, and struck George Morrow on the back of his skull. Blood gushed from a gash and seeped into his collar as Ty grabbed the bloody, swinging buckle end in his other hand and kicked George between the shoulder blades, catching his neck in the loop of the belt, and held George down with one knee and braced himself, heaving on the belt, forcing an unnatural arch on George's upper back until several men pulled at him and someone punched him in the head, when finally he let go and George's face thudded onto the floor.

Dr. Ahmed ran to George's side to give him the help he needed. In my imagination.

You know what my brother needed? He needed me to sever my violent limb, dislocate, amputate, abandon. Because, after a breath's worth of stillness, Ty became Tyandabby, and he vaulted over the counter, scattering tidy rows of plastic cups containing single shots of vodka, rye, and rum. Evaporating alcohol stung my eyes and nose, and I tried to catch the liquid in my hands as it spilled over the counter and through my fingers.

NEAR
MISS

vy turned too fast into the grocery store parking lot, and the Volvo slid on icy, hard-packed snow. She oversteered, clipped a stray grocery cart, and narrowly missed another car. She parked with shaking hands and glanced at her daughter in the passenger seat making a peace sign and pouty lips at her phone. "Lauren! Pay attention!" The blithe selfie on top of a near accident was too much. The fifteen-year-old's online life – a life not under Ivy's control and a universe distant from her own teen years – provoked her. Then again, maybe virtual trouble was better than real-life trouble. Maybe a dick pic was better than an actual dick. She had no advice to offer.

She got out to inspect the damage, and the car dinged as she stood staring at the small rear-panel dent.

"Mom, close the door," Lauren whined. "It's cold."

She hadn't noticed her speed because she'd been silently reckoning her articling student's myriad mistakes on the Melanchuk file. As she stared, she came up with a plan: groceries, drop Lauren off at her father's, file insurance claim on way to office, fix Melanchuk file, work out, sleep, write student's performance review Sunday morning, late brunch with junior partner, long run, rice bowl, to bed with Louise Penny and Chief Inspector Gamache.

She walked briskly ahead of Lauren, mentally mapping out the most efficient route through the store and avoiding eye contact with a tall, rough-looking man who was smoking near the entrance. As the automatic doors shushed open, she heard behind her, "Hey. Hey, Ivy."

The man wore a grubby, red plaid jacket, greasy jeans, and old steel-toed boots. His hair was lank. He was looking at Lauren.

"Stop that," said Ivy. "Don't look at her."

"Ivy? Is that you? It's me, Eric. Eric Althouse. No offence. I thought she was you." He pointed at Lauren. "What happened to your hair? Can you lend me some money?"

"Excuse me?" Ivy touched her expensively highlighted bob.

"Mom, what's happening?"

The automatic doors kissed closed and shushed open as Ivy dithered. Still keyed up from the near accident, she wasn't prepared for a reunion with an old high school friend. Eric was as gangly as she remembered. His long arms hovered cautiously as she hugged him, resting her head under his chin. He smelled like campfire.

Eric bags his rusty Chevette while Ivy balances on Jenn's lap, one hand gripping the door handle, the other elbow braced against the driver's seat, Pepsi slush in hand. Her parents never buy junk food, but she has a little spending money for her sleepover at Jenn's. "Be smart," they said. The whole idea is not to be smart for once. The car judders and skids along a gravel road far south of her family's farm. They share the back seat with two stereo speakers and a subwoofer and all the windows are rolled down, whipping their hair into improbable shapes, and she can't hear her own laughter over the music. The feeling of joy is so complete and full she believes it will escape her if she doesn't make an effort to contain it. The effort almost makes her cry.

Eric overshoots the approach to the farmyard, a treed patch on otherwise flat, bare fields, not yet seeded. "Hold on," he shouts as he pulls the e-brake and makes the car spin neatly.

"Wow, 180 degrees," she says, but luckily no one hears her. Why bring math into it? This is her first real party and she wants to be cool, but it's hard to be cool when you get the best grades in your class and go to church every Sunday with your family. And the rundown farmyard is creepy. Abandoned machinery and rows of overgrown caragana, poplar, and spruce frame the place, and at its centre is what appears to be a haunted house, white paint peeling, plywood in a second-storey window. A few bright, tough tulips break through the matted grass around the foundation. Where there was once a lawn or garden stands a firepit surrounded by folding lawn chairs, old tractor seats rooted in the ground, and a high-backed couch belching stuffing on which Trent sits.

Everyone knows Trent. He's old, maybe twenty-four, twenty-five. He rents a house in town which functions as a middle finger to the school across the street. Empty beer bottles litter his front dandelion patch and Christmas lights twinkle year-round, drooping from the soffits. She's heard he "pulls beer" for kids. She pictures him pulling a child's red wagon full of beer but is pretty sure that's not how it works. Trent has his arm around Amber, a girl in her grade who she doesn't like very much. It's mutual. The giant plastic cup in Amber's small hands makes her look even tinier than she is.

Eric parks near the house alongside a few trucks. Jenn says, "Here, quick," and pours clear alcohol from a bottle with a cute polar bear on the label into Ivy's Pepsi slush. The front seats of the Chevette don't fold down any more, so Ivy squeezes between the upright seat and the door frame. Her foot catches on a dangling seat belt, and she flops onto the ground. Through a feat of athleticism, she saves her drink.

"Fucking A," shouts Trent from the couch. "Doesn't spill a drop. She's got her fucking priorities straight." He turns to Amber and says, "Not like you, Spilly," and tickles her until a splash of brown liquid sloshes onto the couch.

The tickling makes Ivy uncomfortable and so does the thought of sitting on that gross couch, but Jenn plops down next to Trent. He lays a hairy arm around her shoulders. Ivy hangs back with Eric and his girlfriend, Trish — they're more Jenn's friends than hers and older, in grade twelve. She pretends to be interested in the stereo system Eric sets up in the hatchback, then follows them to the firepit to the bouncy notes of Depeche Mode's "Personal Jesus."

Trent bellows, "Althouse, what's with the electronic shit?"

"They're English," says Eric. "I like it."

"You're forgiven, but only because your grandma's old place is the perfect party spot. And you brought girls." Trent rises from the couch, beer bottle sandwiched between prayer hands, and bows.

Trish flops into a fraying lawn chair, and Eric stands beside her, prying caps off two beers with his Bic lighter. Ivy picks a tractor seat next to Trish. She'd like to see if it spins on its post, but she has to be mature, like a real teenager. She sips her spiked slush through a straw. It tastes disgusting and that must show on her face, because Eric offers her his dimples as he angles onto Trish's lap. "Will it hold?" he asks, clowning, long skinny legs in the air. The lawn chair squawks. "Will it?" Trish's laugh is deep and bronchial.

"Althouse," says Trent. He looks annoyed. Probably because he isn't the centre of attention. Her cousin Derek gets that way. "I saw your grandma walking down the street the other day."

He mimics a hunched shuffle. "She's bald, man. I thought only dudes went bald."

Eric disentangles himself and stands, chest forward, and Trent lunges and big-brothers him into a rough chokehold. "Can't take a fucking joke?" And both crash onto the ground at Ivy's feet. She hugs her knees in tight, making herself as small as possible. Trent gets up chuckling, a complete jerk. Eric, red-faced, brushes grass and dirt out of his hair.

Eric lives with his Grandma Pederson in one of the seniors' bungalows in town because his parents died in a car accident last fall. Her first funeral. She and her family had to sit in overflow in the church basement facing a wall with a poster of white, bearded Jesus teaching the children. The poster was surrounded by Sunday school macaroni art. As the pastor's words buzzed through one blown speaker in the corner, she read and reread the poster's Bible verse. *Let the little children come to me, and do not hinder them, for the kingdom of heaven belongs to such as these.* "Such as these." It had to be the parents who were doing the hindering in this scenario and Eric would probably be overjoyed to have his own hinderers back.

"Who are you?" Trent calls. He waits for an answer, wiping dirt off the rim of his beer bottle.

"Ivy." She unfolds her legs and pivots back and forth on her tractor seat.

"Like the stuff that creeps up walls?"

"Yeah."

"I like it. Fucking Ivy. Girl-who-doesn't-spill. Rhymes almost." He looks around the circle and taps his chest. "I'm a fucking poet!" He turns his attention back to her and says, "You won't tell anyone about our secret party spot here, will you? You don't spill, do you, Ivy?"

Ivy shakes her head.

"Good girl." He drinks the last from his bottle and throws it into the trees. Glass shatters.

Eric talked unceasingly on the drive to Ivy's tidy new sub-division. The dimples, friendliness, and charisma were the same; the filth, homelessness, and sunken cheeks were new. Eric wasn't shy about how he'd gotten there. He told her and Lauren that after high school he'd lost his grandma, flunked out of university, found work in Lloydminster, had a serious girlfriend, lost time and girlfriend in Vancouver, got in some drug trouble, fracked in Fort McMurray, drugs again, more trouble, Calgary, homeless shelter. "Then my auntie tells me on Facebook that Grandma Pederson's old place has been for sale since last Christmas. No one else wants it, so I figure I'll squat there until the government gives it to me, but I've got to get there somehow. Will you give me a ride?"

"Squatter's rights aren't a thing in Saskatchewan," said Lauren from the back seat.

"She's right, more or less," said Ivy, glancing at Lauren through the rear-view mirror. "Don't ask me how she knows that."

By the time she pulled into her garage, she had a new plan. Adjustments to the schedule were necessary. She'd file the SGI claim Monday and write her student's review later in the week, squeeze in the brunch, the run, and Melanchuk file before Monday.

Laundry first while Eric showered and took a nap. As

instructed, he'd left his dirty clothes in a basket outside the spare bedroom so, in rubber gloves and not looking too closely, she dumped the basket into the washer and started a load set to scalding. Then she found the listing for the old Pederson place. The price was tragically low, reduced twice. She contacted her bank, her lawyer, and the real estate office – the agent would meet her at the yard at five o'clock. They had four hours. She packed a suitcase full of clothes Richard had left behind. She boxed up an extra set of dishes she'd gotten at her wedding and never liked, a few pots and pans, assorted household supplies. She filled a cooler with food and found a card table, two folding chairs, an inflatable mattress, a pillow, and a sleeping bag. How these possessions had escaped last year's Kondo treatment, she wasn't sure. She enlisted Lauren to shoehorn it all into the Volvo.

Lauren hadn't touched her phone despite a near constant pinging from her back pants pocket; for the first time in months, she had her daughter's full attention. It only took picking up a homeless man and buying him a house. "Don't ever drink or do drugs," she advised, not wanting to waste the opportunity.

The sun sinks behind the trees and people continue to arrive at the party – apparently not that big a secret. Jenn is sitting on some out-of-town guy's lap, a beer bottle in her hand. Everyone is laughing and shouting. Small groups form and break up and reform in the gathering darkness outside the light of the fire. Ivy continues to swivel on her tractor seat, listening to stories of victory, near misses, fights, "that cunt." Her slush doesn't taste so bad near the end. She tosses her empty cup into the fire and watches the waxy cardboard cringe. She stands and lurches to the lip of the fire. "Whoopsie." She wanders around the yard looking for Eric or Trish. Where'd they go? Something's wrong with her eyes. Is Todd walking around with antlers on his head? Has Amber taken off her shirt? So funny. Everyone laughs and laughs. People are calling her Whoopsie for some reason.

She's on the front steps of the house. She has to pee. The door's locked. She high-steps through the matted grass, falls, gets up, walks carefully, carefully to the fire, finds Jenn, still on out-of-town-guy lap, pulls on Jenn's arm, stage whispers, "Jenn. I didn't know you could even lock a farmhouse." So funny. "Jenn. I'm serious." She holds Jenn by both arms now, staring into her eyes, sincere, like two people in a movie. "Where do I pee?" They laugh and Jenn points to the trees.

Ivy was checking items off her list at the kitchen island when Eric appeared wearing Richard's old bathrobe. The hem ended well above his knees, calling to mind a sickly Roman legionnaire. "Don't laugh," he said.

"How could I? You look so distinguished." When was the last time she'd teased a grown man? Maybe Richard? Early on? About his Star Trek collection? If she hadn't, she should've.

Lauren shouted from the entryway, "That's all of it, Mom." She stepped into the kitchen and stared at her father's old robe, Eric's skinny legs, and her mother presiding over it all. Ivy couldn't interpret her expression.

"Ivy," said Eric, tugging at the robe, "this is the cleanest fucking house I've ever seen. Excuse my French, Lauren; it could be in a magazine though."

"Yeah, she's totally OCD," said Lauren.

Was she obsessive or compulsive or disordered? Richard

had called her a control freak. But if she wasn't in control, who would be? Certainly not Richard or Eric. Not Lauren, not yet. Maybe soon though. She was already diagnosing her mother with a mental disorder. *Seam ripper.* Ivy fled upstairs to find it. Eric could have the robe, along with the rest of Richard's abandoned clothes, but he'd need a seam ripper to let out the hems.

An hour later, she dropped Lauren off at her dad's with the reminder, "Even if your father says you can go to that party tonight, you cannot." She stirred the air with her index finger. "And maybe don't tell him about all this."

"As if." Lauren turned halfway up the walk and shouted, "Good luck, Eric!"

Eric waved back. "That's a good girl you've got there."

Lauren was a good girl and hadn't questioned why her mother was doing what she was doing. That would come later. And she knew Lauren wouldn't tell Richard anything, hadn't needed to ask. Lauren had advanced secret-keeping skills. She understood when to keep things to herself.

Ivy forced her shoulders down and put on one of the few CDs she hadn't sacrificed to Kondo. They drove out of the city accompanied by Radiohead's *OK Computer.*

"I'm going to pay you back, you know," said Eric as he reclined the seat as far back as it would go and closed his eyes. "I love this album. They're English. I like English bands."

"I remember."

She looked out at the straight road ahead and the clean fields on either side, blond stubble visible above the snow. Eric's hair was the same colour as the straw. Wispy, clean, and uncut as if he were a small child, as if it was his first growth. *Such as these.*

She peers into the darkness, teetering for a moment at the edge of the caragana bush, then crashes in, scratching her arms on branches covered in new buds. The three-quarter moon casts some light, and she wanders between rows of poplar and spruce and over fallen deadwood until she can't see the party anymore, can't hear the voices around the fire, only the music. Metallica now. Eric must've lost control of the stereo. She draws down her jeans and underwear, squats, and pees, steadying herself with a palm on a tree trunk. She's dizzy so she rests in her squat after she's finished to drip dry. Her hand is covered in spruce sap, and she opens and closes it a few times, enjoying the pull on her skin. A dry branch snaps.

Trent holds out his arm as if to calm a wild animal. "Nature calls?" Mortified, she tugs at her jeans, crouching in an attempt to hide herself, but he says, "Hold on," and grabs her arm. "Let's talk." He yanks her to him and kisses her face and neck. She pushes at his chest and strains her face away from his. He shoves her onto the ground. She scrambles backwards. Then he's on top of her. Spruce needles prick her bare thighs. A screeching sound comes out of her. He clamps a hard hand over her mouth. It smells of dill pickle chips. His knees wedge between her legs.

Then she hears a heavy thud and feels something wet on her face and he's off her. She breathes again, rakes a sleeve across her mouth, and clambers to her feet, yanking up her jeans. She hears a crack, like the sound of wood snapping in a fire and looks over to where Trent writhes on the dark ground, holding his arm to his chest. Eric stands tall above him. "I saw him follow you into the trees, and I had a bad feeling."

The Pederson place looked little like it used to. It was still surrounded by spruce and poplar, but much of the deadwood had been cleared and the caragana ripped out, allowing the farmyard to breath again. The rusty machinery had been hauled away, and there was no evidence of a firepit, but in Ivy's imagination it still smouldered under the deer- and jackrabbit-tracked snow. The house was repainted a dark blue and the windows had been replaced – a couple of freelance writers from Toronto had fixed it up, lured by the low cost of living. "But you've got to really like one another or be stubborn as hell," said the indiscreet real estate agent. "Every farm couple knows that."

After the paper signing, Ivy and Eric sat together at the card table in the kitchen. He had a smoke – it *was* his house – and she admitted she owed him, told him how she felt about what he'd done for her. "You looked like an avenging angel."

"I'm sorry that happened to you, Ivy, but I don't remember it. I broke some guy's arm?" He shared his dimples. He couldn't hide his delight with the house. "You sure it was me?"

"Why did you think I bought you this house?"

"Old friends?"

How could he not remember? This episode had shaped everything. For him it was, what, another forgotten party, another forgotten fight? How much violence had he seen? Which day was it that finally set him onto his own set of rails? Or were there too many? Her anger subsided. While still wishing a memory on him, she imagined a different past for him, and a future full of purpose: he'd be an elementary-school teacher, a kind father of daughters, a good-humoured husband, a man who made other people happy and feel safe.

She drove home from the farmyard that night with the window open, allowing February cold to keep her awake while Thom Yorke sang, *You don't remember! You don't remember!* like he knew her or was her. According to the ubiquitous green sign illuminated in the headlights, the next town offered the only service she needed. She pulled off the highway and angle-parked in front of a two-storey building on Main Street with grey asphalt shingles for siding and neon signage confirming HOTEL and OFF-SALE. Her yesterday self would never have entered a place like this, but today she paid for a room, then went to the bar and ordered fries with gravy and a beer, all from the same person. He was probably the cook too. The fries were delicious, the beer disgusting, and the staring of the other patrons uninhibited. The staring, rather than intimidating her – which may or may not have been the intention – made her feel like an exotic stranger, as if these weren't actually her people. But she kept to herself, remembering the joy she'd kept tamped down in Eric's Chevette, the fear and sadness she'd avoided in the church basement, the shrinking girl on a tractor seat. She'd always been this contained, controlled thing. Maybe what she'd thought of as her most life-changing moment had just been another moment among many. A memorable near miss, but still, just one moment.

Finally, full and exhausted, she trudged upstairs, identifying images in each worn rubber stair tread. Her room above the bar was narrow, maybe twice the width of its lone twin bed. In the strip of non-bed space were a chair upholstered in the same red vinyl as the bar stools, a sink by the lace-curtained window, and a lamp on a small bedside table. After a visit to the bathroom down the hall, there was nothing to do but wash her face, take off her boots, and crawl under the cool top sheet and fraying wool blanket. She appreciated the exquisite lack of choice, the room's clarity of purpose: *sleep, already.* As she reached to turn off the lamp, she noticed a sticky ring on the bedside table and a brown stain on the doily underneath the lamp. She hadn't pulled up the mattress and sheets to check for bedbugs like she had in every boutique hotel, guest bedroom, and berth in which she'd ever slept. She switched off the light and wondered why she'd done that all those years. She'd never found a single one.

FOREIGN CONDITIONS

Alex wants the pain to go away. He climbs worn marble stairs to his hotel room on the fourth floor, bursitis flare-up in knee, new taupe walking shoes pinching hot, swollen feet. In the shoe store a few days before they left on their first ever European vacation, he'd told Trudy the taupe shoes made him look like an old man, and she'd said, "If the shoe fits!" Surprised to hear her laugh again – she hadn't much since Paul died the previous summer – he'd bought the damn things. By the third landing, his nostrils flare wide to accommodate the increased oxygen exchange, but he will not pant. The Roman hotel doesn't have an elevator, and some men in the tour group complained and were moved to rooms on the ground floor. He unlocks the door to his room, breathing heavily. The bed is freshly made up in light, white bedding, which he imagines dark-eyed Italian maids airing while gossiping about the fit and dignified *signore* who sleeps in this room. *The one with the old man shoes?* Sì, *him.*

He pries off his shoes and pushes open the casement windows overlooking a small square, marvelling that there are no screens. If you don't need to worry about mosquitoes, what other miserable facts of life don't have to concern you? He likes to think the people here – his lovely maids – live a carefree existence. He wishes it for them. But no people is free of cares, and no place can ease pain. Despite Trudy's determination that a European Wonders! tour might jar their grief loose, his is still thistle-rooted somewhere behind his sternum, and, in order to avoid her relentless itinerary this afternoon, he said he needed a nap, claimed vacations were for relaxing. He doesn't think that; he doesn't know what they're for. Other than camping trips when Paul was a boy and a few winter sun vacations in recent years, they haven't travelled much. In his limited experience, vacations were for worrying about the state of the farm in his absence and now also for tending his grief thistle under foreign conditions.

A chubby tourist slumps on the stone lip of the fountain in the centre of the square, nursing her foot. Minus the tourist, it's a beautiful view – aged amber walls, shutters artfully askew, wrought-iron balconies, charming cafes, fountain – a view the rest of the tour group will not enjoy from their ground floor rooms. *Spoiled weaklings.* The memory of his outburst from the night before makes him wince with shame. *Get over it, Alex.* Trudy was sitting on the bed writing postcards while he paced, deriding their fellow tour members for refusing to climb a few stairs.

"Get over it, Alex. They don't want to have a heart attack on vacation," Trudy said. "Maybe they didn't buy extra health insurance."

"We're becoming a nation of spoiled weaklings. Climbing a few stairs? What would their fathers have thought? What kind of example are they setting for our country? For their children?"

"You forget their grandchildren."

He stopped pacing, turned to his wife, embarrassed by his misplaced passion. These were more sentences than he'd managed to string together since they'd begun their tour in Paris two weeks ago. The Eiffel Tower and *Mona Lisa* combined had received less commentary.

Trudy's fingers were tracing the naked Matisse dancers on her favourite new skirt. He wasn't so sure about the skirt but had learned long ago to keep these kinds of opinions to himself. They would never have grandchildren. Then Trudy straightened her back. "On the bright side, they think we're Americans. Canada's reputation is safe!" Such faith in bright sides, convinced there exists a solution to every problem.

He turns away from the square and lies down, careful not to disturb the immaculate bedding. Stretched out on his back with his hands folded on his chest, he closes his eyes and sees Paul, lying in the same attitude, orange-faced in the embalmer's makeup. He rolls onto his side, pulls his knees up to his chest, and covers his eyes with his fists. He's taken to these self-soothing postures of childhood. He curls around his thistle root and falls asleep to the sound of clattering dishes and chatter from the cafe below.

Trudy waits in line to show her prepaid ticket to an unusually cheerful functionary at the Galleria Borghese. The other members of the European Wonders! tour group are having their pictures taken on the Spanish Steps or tramping around the Colosseum while Alex naps at the hotel. She told him they had siestas in Spain, not Italy, but he said vacations were for relaxing. Ridiculous. She passes through the ticket-taking and security gates without any exhibitions of animosity. The cool quiet and airiness of the Borghese compares favourably to the teeming Vatican that morning, the shuffling hoard progressing through miles of spectacular rooms, each wall covered in paintings or frescoes and every ceiling ornately decorated. Whenever she stopped to admire the art some idiot would walk right into her. The last time it happened, their fanny packs bumped in a way that felt too familiar. They were like two monsters who mated by bumping bumps. After a short gestation period, out from her fanny pack would emerge a new monster, fully formed, itinerary in hand, ready to start its own slow, sweaty shuffle to the Sistine Chapel, which must have been beautiful, but now she only remembers the rank smell of Alex's sweat and the guards shouting, "No flash! Reverence!"

Had she even looked up? She won't admit to Alex she is disappointed. If she's honest, the whole European tour has been an expensive disappointment. It isn't Europe's fault; to expect a place which has caused a fair share of the world's grief to heal theirs is unrealistic. Though she can't remember her reasoning for booking the tour exactly, it had something to do with old Europe's monuments to beauty and history helping put things in perspective. Seems tenuous now as she begrudges Alex his nap. Because of course they've packed their grief, carry-on and oversized, and it bumps along behind them over the old cobblestones.

Glass shatters. From the cafe below, a British woman's voice.

"No, Daniel, don't touch the glass."

"*No, signora. Mi permetta.*"

"*Grazie.* Say thank you, Daniel. Say *grazie* to the nice man."

"*Molte grazie, signore.*" A boy's voice.

"*Prego!* You speak *italiano* very good."

"Well done, Daniel," says another man.

"*Molte grazie, signore. Molte grazie,* Dad. *Molte grazie,* Mum." Laughter and clapping.

Alex is awake. He guesses the boy's around eight. Paul at that age was all teeth and worry, neatly parted hair. He'd been a polite kid too.

"*Un gelato per bambino!*"

"Did you hear that, Daniel?" says the mother. "He's bringing ice cream."

"I understood him. Dad, if I dropped my water glass in that place –"

"The Pantheon."

"The water would disappear into those holes in the floor, right?"

"That's right."

"Then where does the water go?"

"There are probably drainage pipes that carry it to the sewer system."

"So when it rains, it comes in through that big hole in the ceiling –"

"The oculus."

"The octopus."

"Oculus."

"When it rains, the rain falls on the floor and goes into those little holes and then into the pipes and then into the sewer system?"

"Yes, I think so. How many holes did you find?"

"Loads."

"It says here that there are twenty-four."

"Can we go back? I need to find them all. Please."

"After your ice cream."

Alex rolls out of bed and sticks his head out the window but can't see the family under the umbrella. Paul had been a collector too: comics, rocks, nail clippings, classmates' insults, addictions. Alex had not been as attentive as this father. Trudy always told him his love language was work – she talked like that sometimes – and maybe it's true. But it's also true he loved the work itself and found it easy to put in the long hours the farm required. He sees it now: he was as sensitive to weather, soil conditions, ripeness, feed quality, calving stages, as he was ignorant of his son. He had Paul do chores, knowing that farming was not his calling but assuming everyone found their own work eventually, and he could apply farming principles to that thing. Did boys need more than industriousness in a father? He loved his boy but shouldn't he have tried to understand him? Or maybe there was nothing he could have done. Paul had Trudy too – her love languages were many – and he'd still taken all those pills.

Trudy was right. He should get out of the hotel and take a look around. At least try. He finds the Pantheon on his map, pulls on his socks and shoes, and descends – knee aching, shoes rubbing – to the lobby. He walks out into the square, hoping to see the family in the cafe, but they've already left.

But Trudy won't give up on this vacation like a certain napper she could name. The museum used to be the Borghese family villa, some of the art collected by a cardinal nephew, and she forces herself to imagine what it must have been like to live there. She meanders through the beautiful, high-ceilinged rooms slowly and in no particular order, like a bored Borghese might, and loses track of time staring at an intricate floor mosaic. She stands in front of some paintings for a long time, moving close to the canvases then far away. Others she only glances at. That old thing? But when she steps into a room and sees a young man stretching up from a plinth in the middle of the room, twisted in action and so lifelike, she blurts, "Oh," then laughs at herself and puts a hand up to cover her mouth. She's back to being Trudy from the farm. A girl sitting on a stool nearby smiles at her sketch pad.

Trudy comes closer. The young man's brow is furrowed in concentration and anger; his lips sucked in with effort. He's about to hurl a stone in a sling, his body torqued for leverage. Another David. She finds the label on a nearby wall: *David, Bernini Gian Lorenzo, 1623, Marmo.* This David is beautiful in a way unlike the more famous one in Florence. Instead of looking like an excuse to sculpt the perfect body of a vanquishing hero, this David is in the middle of the action, fighting for his life. Instead of a slingshot hanging limply down his back, fresh from killing Goliath, this David's sling is primed. This David doesn't know what the outcome will be.

Did Paul know the outcome of taking all those drugs? They received the news of his death from an officer in the local RCMP detachment who'd driven onto their yard during lunch on a hot July day. Before the officer could tell them his purpose, she had invited him in for an egg-salad sandwich.

They arranged for Paul's body to be shipped home from Vancouver and buried him in the family cemetery on the south quarter. She felt guilty about that – all he ever wanted was to get out – but Alex said Paul had given up on choices. She supposes he's right, but they haven't picked a headstone yet. They can't find the words. Neither for the discussion nor the epitaph.

Trudy circles the statue, examining David from every angle. The folds in the skin at his side where he's bent, ready to fight. His strong shoulders. The piece of cloth twisted around his body. His knees and toes, the discarded armour at his feet. It seems perfectly natural to be fighting naked – fighting your way out of life as you fought your way in. As she peers at his face, the girl on the stool asks if she speaks English. Rust-throated, Trudy croaks, "Yes, dear."

"That's Bernini's face." Her voice is full of wonder.

"Whose?"

The girl drags her stool to new spot, not hearing the question, while Trudy's menopausal brain catches up: the sculptor modelled David's face on his own. That concentrated anger was the artist's. How did it feel to spend hours chiselling out your own face? What would you learn?

During the last of Paul's rare visits home, he'd told her, "Stop staring. Jesus. What are you looking at?"

She has always wished for a one-way mirror between herself and the world, allowing her to look at it unobserved – released from social conventions – for as long as she liked. When the world looked back, it would see itself, maybe preen a little, maybe reflect. With that one-way mirror she would have examined her son from every angle, like she is this David, in order to learn and understand, do and say the right things. Perhaps it would have given Paul enough time to examine his own face and do the same. *What are you looking at?* Or maybe they all – mothers, fathers, children – required different tools: chisels, say, and marble. Subtracting until they found themselves in stone.

The cobblestones make Alex feel like he's just learned to walk. Every step requires attention. Passing shops, he smells tobacco, coffee, overripe fruit. He avoids other wobbly tourists. When he arrives at a large square, there's no mistaking the Pantheon. The afternoon sun is hot, and he heads for the columns to get into their shade, pausing to let his eyes adjust before stepping past the bronze doors, the entrance big enough to drive a tractor through. He's blinded by a beam of sunlight and moves a few steps then looks up. A column of dust-swirled light angles through a circular hole in the domed ceiling, like the slant of light from the fill hole in an empty grain bin. The "octopus" is beautiful. He looks down at the marble floor set in geometric patterns. He paces with his hands behind his back, tracing the smoky swirls in the marble with his eyes. When he finds the first set of holes in the floor, he lowers himself slowly onto one knee and runs his hand over the cool surface. The holes are in a set of four ovals like an evenly plucked daisy.

"Over here!" Alex looks up at the familiar voice. Daniel is pointing down at him. "*Buongiorno.* May I look at those?"

Alex pushes on his knee, sending a flare of pain up his thigh. "Could you?" he asks the boy, holding out his hand. Daniel plants his feet and pulls on Alex's arm, providing enough support for him to stand. "Thank you, son." He places a hand on the boy's bony shoulder.

"*Prego, signore.*" Daniel smooths down an imaginary stray hair. "I'm strong."

"I see that." Alex gestures at the marble floor. "Help yourself."

"Is he bothering you?" says the boy's mother as she and the father catch up to their son. "Daniel, what do you say?"

"*Molte grazie, signore.*"

"You're welcome. *Prego*," says Alex experimentally. He likes the sound of Italian, even out of his own mouth. "Would you help me find the rest?"

As Daniel guides him to all the holes, Alex crouches like a child. He shares the boy's wonder at the craft, industry, and ingenuity of the ancient building. The oculus a solution to the problem of light, the drainage holes a solution to the problem of rain, the beauty of the whole a solution to the problem of the gods.

INTERSTICES

Lisa tugged her attention away from the ruminating yaks, jotted one last line in her notebook, stood, and yawned. Her ears popped. Victory! She patted her body up and down in her lightweight yet warm yet wicking gear and found her cell zipped up in a thigh pocket. She tweeted. *@lisabilanski Ears popped for first time since landing in Kathmandu! #everest #miracles*

Where had Karl gone?

Must have carried on without her. Because he'd found out what she'd done? Because he hated her? She couldn't stop the steady, slicing anxiety of uncertainty. Uncertainty over how much Karl knew, what cheating on Karl for the first time ever in their marriage meant, whether her current obsequiousness with Karl was the right tone to take while harbouring a secret betrayal, how she was going to pull off a fresh Everest story. This was the biggest assignment of her adventure-travel writing career, but what was there left to say about Everest? The trip had started out all wrong. She usually tagged along with Karl and his buddies on their hiking-cycling-climbing-trekking trips – like a little sister – then wrote about it. This time it was she who'd come up with the adventure and Karl who was along for the ride. Though an expedition discount for being the team's in-house doctor had been his idea, he would never have chosen Everest: too commercial, too unseemly. In her pitch to *Outings Magazine*, he'd suggested she employ the term "shenanigans" to describe the Everest scene. Consequently, all this worrying and sucking up she was doing was unseemly. Rooted in shenanigans.

The narrow streets of Namche wound and pitched. She tripped on a raised cobblestone. What a fraud she was. The trek had gone smoothly so far, and she was acclimatizing well, despite her cold and these weird backaches — the rest in Namche was helping — but they were only halfway. Halfway to base camp; halfway to starting. And she was not a natural climber, never would be. She blamed it on her legs which went on forever — an advantage in most of life's corners, but not this one. She sneezed, pausing in the street in front of a café. *@lisabilanski Thank you @Himalayan_Java! Caffeine addiction follows you all over the world.* Opposite was a bazaar stall selling T-shirts that shouted *I CLIMBED EVEREST!* in many languages. She smoothed the balled-up tissue in her fist and blew her nose for the thousandth time. Ears plugged. Back into her conch shell.

"Bit presumptuous to buy a T-shirt now, don't you think?"

She turned. There he was. "Oh, come on!" She slapped him playfully on his chest. Her laugh, theatrical.

"What's the matter?"

"My ears! Hey, Karl, check this out." She hopped on one foot, head at an angle, index finger waggling in her ear. "Do I look like I'm ready for reality dance television?" She got her chest into it. "Am I krumping?"

"What?" Karl took a step away from her. He never watched television. She gave up on her ears and the performance and slipped her arm into his. They meandered down the street browsing the vendors' stalls with their nutty mix of hand-crafted and mass-produced: embroidered handbags hung over *The Hangover III;* traditional wool hats accessorized with acid-green shower sandals; malodorous hand-knit sweaters cushioned purple-maned toy ponies. And any piece of climbing gear you might need just in case ... *@lisabilanski Oops, forgot to pack a jacket to climb Everest. Good thing I can buy anything anywhere!*

"Texting your boyfriend?"

"What? What do you mean? No."

"You have the thumbs of a teenager."

"The magazine retweets some of them. And my followers are eager to read about my progress. Why are you looking at me like that? They are." Karl pulled his camera out of his backpack. "Did you get any good ones?"

"Yeah, not bad," he said, scrolling through pictures, stopping at one of an old couple in the bazaar. "See how their faces are so weathered, surrounded by all these colours? Great tension." He paused at another photo of a grubby, gorgeous young man, a herder maybe, staring solemnly at the camera. He had taken up photography lately and, like everything, had subdued and conquered it. Karl was not a dabbler.

"Could I use them for my article?" A jewellery stall up ahead caught her eye. "Sorry for losing you back there."

"You lost me."

"Sort of."

"No, I mean what are you talking about?"

She had no idea. What was her story? What was the angle? *Aging, childless writer climbs Everest, endears husband?* She was turning forty next year. There were a few other options. *Middle-aged fraud dies on Everest. Woman clings to rocks, marriage. Mid-life crisis, avalanche triggered on Everest. Cheater cheats Everest, husband, readers.* She wandered over to the jewellery stall.

"Look at these. Karl?" His camera was pointing up at criss-crossed prayer flags strung from second storeys and rooftops. "Karl?" He sauntered over, staring at his viewfinder, negotiating the cobblestones deftly. She pointed to the vendor's display of vases, pendants, earrings, rings. There were fish on every one, in circling pairs, arched and face-to-face. Sometimes they chased one another, head to tail. Small intervals between them.

"Carp," he said.

"The fishes symbol good fortune, freedom, no fear," said the man behind the table. He was wearing a wool hat, the strings of which hung alongside his white beard, and a Toronto Raptors sweatshirt. "You have many children."

Was it a question? Lisa asked how much for a pendant. She pulled a wad of rupees from a hidden pocket-within-a-pocket, along with used tissues, one of which fell and did a tumbleweed down the street. She'd read she should haggle but paid the asking price.

"No kids yet, but I love basketball," she said pointing to his sweatshirt and giving a thumbs-up. He looked down at the logo, confused. She turned away, ran a finger over her pendant with its relief of two fish, examining their bodies that curved in towards each other. Almost kissing.

When she looked up, Karl was gone.

They stalked, post-argument, toward the expedition team's mess hall for another base camp supper. They would eat with purpose this time, after two weeks' acclimatization, preparing for the climb up the Khumbu Icefall the next day. She stumbled on an expended oxygen tank and grabbed Karl's arm to stop herself from diving into the sharp rocks.

"It's going to get tougher than this, Lisa."

Babying relationship, body, job, and guilt all at once was proving unsustainable at base camp. She had to prioritize. Her reasoning was this. She had made a mistake, which would not be repeated. Nobody was hurt. She could always worry about it later. The story was the thing. Plus, Karl was being an ass. She pulled herself up to her full height so she could see the top of his head. "Your bald spot's the size of a toonie now, Karl."

He yanked a fleece beanie out of his pocket and crammed it onto his head.

She grimaced at the stench carried on the dusty, springtime gusts. Things that surprised on Everest expedition, Number 72: the intermittent smell of human shit. Her editor had emailed and asked her to cut out the "moody shit" in her tweets. "Find the dirt!" You'd think she could find some dirt among all these people. They milled about, jabbering into mobile phones, carrying video cameras, toting strappy, colourful gear to and fro. But they refused to do anything newsworthy: no cholera outbreak, no fist fights with the Sherpa, no orgies. *@lisabilanski Base camp smells of shit.*

The mess hall was a canvas tent with two gritty plastic patio tables and enough matching chairs to seat the nine team members. Near the entrance, the lone Nepalese woman on the expedition's support staff piled gelatinous bean stew onto tin plates. The Sherpa porters ate elsewhere. They didn't like the food? The company? What was not to like? Ha! There was Jean-Pierre, the unnecessarily handsome Québécois expedition leader, sitting at the far table. He caught sight of them and, as usual, saluted. *Pourquoi?* It was true Karl could come off a touch militaristic: the posture, the tidiness, the self-discipline, the humourlessness. She wasn't laughing anyway. Karl picked the empty table, and Danielle and Tristan joined them. Danielle was from the Yukon, forty-five, wiry, small, tough, with a weakness for Tristan, the thirty-two-year-old Calgary CFO, who noted upon sitting, "I'm so fucking stoked about the icefall tomorrow. What the fuck is this? Is it edible?"

Lisa smirked and Karl's posture stiffened beyond military. Their argument had been about Tristan who, by virtue of being Karl's exact opposite, had managed to push all his buttons over the preceding weeks. This had led Karl, normally and compassionately reserving of his high standards for himself and Lisa, to snipe, "It's a miracle Tristan managed to climb to the top of the monetary heap, let alone base camp." Which led Lisa to get weird about it, to take it personally, and defend Tristan on a number of grounds she could only guess at. It had gone downhill from there.

"Just eat it," said Danielle grinning.

"Yes, Mommy." Tristan took a forkful. "This is shit." He swallowed. "And I'd kill for a bottle of Bordeaux."

He had a point.

Austerity was typical of Karl's enthusiasms, the ones she had subsequently adopted as her own. Her first exposure had been a Jasper-to-Banff bike trip with Karl's cycling club one Labour Day long weekend. They were still dating then; she'd married him anyway. Snow had pelted them at the Columbia Icefields and shrouded their two-man tent-coffin in the mornings. She hadn't trained beforehand, thinking biking to and from work fifteen minutes each way might do the trick, so there she was, dying at the back of the pack with another fresh and determined girlfriend. Every time they caught up with the rest of the group for a carb break, Karl and Trevor, his long-time cycling partner, had already started out again. As she wobbled into the campsite at the end of the day, Karl and Trevor were chatting and laughing over a pot of chili, oblivious to her presence. She always felt invisible around those two. When Karl finally noticed her, he pointed to the five-gallon water jug and said, "Make sure to hydrate!" Chili and water. No beer, no wine, no bread, no butter, no music, no bed. Nothing to obliterate the pain in her butt or the sweat freezing up her back. She ate her chili standing up. The temperature had been colder than Everest base camp. And of course, not to forget all the years declining drinks at dinner parties as they tried for a baby – the hosts, in the last few years, cringing when they offered. She was due for a drink.

"Oh my god, you privileged little –" Danielle paused. "Tristan! What is it?" Tristan was silent. His face red. He fumbled with an inside jacket pocket.

"Can you speak?" Lisa asked, words tumbling. Tristan pointed frantically at his pocket. She worked on the zipper which was caught. She almost had it. Karl was over the table and shoved her away. She fell backwards in her chair, bouncing off the canvas wall back to upright. Stitches ripped and something fell. Karl dove under the table, grabbed the object and jabbed it into Tristan's thigh. Tristan gasped, coughed, and sighed. A tear pioneered a straight path down his cheek. "Fuck me," he croaked.

Tristan submitted as Karl helped him to his feet, his arm around Karl's shoulder, Karl's arm around Tristan's waist. Danielle followed them out of the tent, fidgeting with unspent adrenaline. Lisa sat, body humming.

Jean-Pierre came to her side. "Tristan, he is in good hands." He placed a hand on her own. "That is the expression?"

"Yes."

Her husband's hands. Not unlike her own, with their long, narrow fingers. His able to make surgical instruments slice and pry and excise; hers merely to type and text. So different from Tristan's, which she remembered interlocked in hers in that Montreal club bathroom. So broad, forcing her fingers farther apart than they wanted to go, an ostentatious ring grinding a bone. But it had felt good. The need. The urgency. She wasn't sure she'd ever experienced that with Karl; their lovemaking, even early on, feeling prescribed, and it had been months since they'd touched each other.

"He is a good doctor." Jean-Pierre was looking at the tent flap where the doctor and patient had exited.

She didn't know where to slot him, with his damp, dark curls and pretty-girl eyes. His sweet, open demeanour and modesty didn't square with her conception of an Everest shark. Ever since meeting him in Montreal for the team's last-minute expedition preparations, she'd been perplexed, puzzled by his earnestness.

"He is a good man," Jean-Pierre said. "You must love him very much."

She felt her pulse bouncing against the cheap plastic table.

"We climb tomorrow. Eat." Jean-Pierre got up and went over to the cook who was sobbing softly. He put a consoling arm around her.

Alone at the table, Lisa realized she was ravenous, but when she picked up her spoon and looked at the bean stew a hot nausea engulfed her. She made the polite, sick person's calculation, grabbed Karl's beanie which had fallen off during the excitement, and vomited into it. She pushed herself up from the table and left the tent. She plopped the sick-beanie into the garbage can outside, then put her shaking hands to their habitual use, patting herself down to find the cell in a breast pocket. *@lisabilanski Overheard on Everest: I'd kill for a bottle of Bordeaux.*

As she waited her turn to cross a gaping crevasse on the Khumbu Icefall, she forced herself to think about something other than her own body with its demands, complaints, and questions, persistent as a toddler. Over the preceding weeks of acclimatizing forays up and down the mountain from base camp her body had pitched a steady whine: *Why? How? Oww! I'm hungry! Pleeeaaase! Why? How? Oww! I'm tired!...* She was keeping up though – no one could say she wasn't. Queen of the Khumbu! Okay, maybe Danielle was Queen of the Khumbu, but Lisa was definitely a princess or maybe a lady-in-waiting. Tristan was shuffling from one foot to the other in front of her, antsy, nibbling at his fingernails and glancing up at the falls and down at the crevasse. But he was still here too, wasn't he? Even Karl had expressed admiration over Tristan's stoic recovery from anaphylaxis. So many surprises waiting on Everest, just not the ones of interest to *Outings Magazine* editors. *Everest climber felled by peanut. Base camp grump grants grudging respect to Everest snowflake. Everest woman claims "body hurts."*

Karl, of course, was out of sight. He was free climbing with some Australians after becoming fed up and signing many waivers: "It's like a conga line up the mountain, Lisa. How can you stand it?" She couldn't join him unless she wanted to be the tragic subject of another writer's headline. And she still hadn't got a story angle. With the exception of the Swede who had died last week – the news had thrilled her editor but wasn't that unusual – there had been no climbing drama: the weather had been relentlessly co-operative and the relations among expeditions and Sherpa guides, exemplary. Just her luck to catch the near perfect climbing season. She adopted Karl's Everest-weary tone. *@lisabilanski Waiting in conga line to cross earth-ripping crevasse.*

It was Tristan's turn. He shoved his raw fingertips into gloves with a wince and crept forward onto the aluminum ladder bridging the crevasse. "You can do it, Tris!" shouted Danielle from behind. Lisa startled and dropped her cell. Tristan jerked back from the ladder. Without turning around he mumbled something and took another step. He had big feet – as he liked to remind everyone, he was "big everywhere" – and his crampons spanned the first two rungs of the ladder. He held onto the ropes at his sides and took the rungs in careful couplets.

Now Lisa's turn. She imagined herself winning an icy, oxygen-light version of Snakes and Ladders as her boot teetered on the middle of the first rung. Despite her height, her boots did not span the rungs. She was narrow from top to bottom, shaped like a stick of licorice, and she feared slipping between them. It had happened before, at least she thought it had; her mistrust of this memory was equal to its clarity. She had been a child, out at a job site with her father, observing him in his hard hat, jabbing at plans laid out on the tailgate of his truck, surrounded by huddling men. CLANG! Dust billowed. The men gaped at her. Her father came running. She looked down and saw she was standing in the tidy square between ladder rungs. Her father shouted, "Get back in the truck!" and swatted her bum. "That ladder could've killed you!" Then he grabbed her and squeezed her in his arms, tight. Back in the cab of the truck she gazed out the back window at her father and the work men. Some of them smiled at her or mimicked relief with a mop of their brow. Some looked at her with pity. Her father's eyes had stayed on the plans.

Hers were on her boots. The sound of cold metal-on-metal, and her breath. She tried to focus only on the next rung, but her sight slipped farther down the snaking crevasse. She wobbled when she saw him. Or rather his margarine-yellow jacket. He was fetal, freshly dead. He'd lost at Snakes and Ladders last week – the Swede from another expedition team. A serac the size of a bungalow had toppled nearby while he was crossing. Reportedly, his last word had been in English, the language of last resort: "Fuck!" She didn't want her last words to end in an exclamation point. A nice solid period perhaps or, even better, mysterious ellipses ... Life was uncertain enough, why tempt fate by climbing Mount Everest? Why had she looked down? Just two more rungs and she was onto solid snow. She exhaled and turned to watch Danielle glide across the ladder smiling at something, Tristan presumably. She let Danielle pass so she could join him. Ahead of them was a sheer, ten-storey ice wall with pinioned ladders. *@lisabilanski Congaed across Khumbu again.* She returned to her body's whiny drone.

At Camp IV, 26,000 feet, Lisa curled up in her sleeping bag and attempted sleep before the summit push at midnight. The wind buffeted their nylon tent and a loose cord outside whipped it in punishment for forgetting to tuck it away. Before Everest, she thought she'd die from shame or embarrassment: choking on a Brussels sprout in a restaurant bathroom, say, or delaying a visit to the doctor because the plum-sized lump was in a delicate spot. Now she realized she was going to die of fear, or at least a combination of fear and embarrassment. But then she wasn't thinking so good. Her last tweet read, *@lisabilanski and so to my sleeping bad*, channelling Pepys and hypoxia. She felt like she would puke. It had to be altitude sickness, but she couldn't tell Karl. She peered out of a tiny slit in her sleeping bag at him. She had to finish this thing. Surprisingly, Danielle was out with altitude sickness, and Tristan was climbing without her. Lisa couldn't imagine what Tristan was thinking right now, alone in his tent, having come to accept Danielle's mothering with a teenager's initial savagery and ultimate total devotion. Karl was lying on his back, eyes closed, hands folded on his chest inside his mummy bag, looking the part.

Rocks clacked and shifted outside and a voice called, "Oy, Karl."

Karl rose from the dead and unzipped the tent. "J-P. Hey."

J-P? Lisa lay still and watched from the small gap in her sleeping bag. Jean-Pierre smiled, hand sharp at right eyebrow. "Bad news. No summit tomorrow. Wind's up." He paused for a few breaths. "Descent at midnight." He said something else and both men glanced over at her.

"She's asleep," said Karl and turned back to Jean-Pierre.

Jean-Pierre reached a hand around the back of Karl's neck and pulled him into a fast, hard kiss. Lisa's insides plummeted as the rest of her remained perched, immobile, on a ledge 26,000 feet into thin air.

She breathed the air of Namche in greedy gulps. The team had returned to rest and mend their bodies before a second, final summit attempt. At least some team members were mending. Despite the relatively luxurious oxygen levels, she walked Namche's streets in shock, feeling like she'd been beaten with a flu stick, both nauseated and sore all over. She recalled the descent from C4 only in brief vignettes. A Sherpa shouting up at her. Tristan letting off a fluency of swear words after a dusting from a fallen serac. Karl's methodical march. Jean-Pierre's curls. The trek from base camp had featured a steady, throbbing headache. With the exception of practical communication, she had barely spoken to anyone, especially Karl, since the kiss – the memory of which seemed uncertain, given her near hypoxia. He'd been solicitous, assuming she was disappointed about not reaching the summit. "Next time," he had said. "We get one more try." She patted herself and found her cell. Her last tweet read *@lisabilanski The old girl's still got a few cards up her sleeve. #everest* She didn't remember writing this. Didn't sound like her. Her editor had stopped emailing.

She passed through the bazaar and spotted the same jewellery vendor in the same Raptors sweatshirt. "Lady! Lady!" he beckoned to her. He gave her an incongruous thumbs-up. "You are lucky?" She remembered her pendant for the first time since buying it. She found it in the third zippered pocket she tried and peered at it closely. She ran her thumb over the relief, tracing the lines of the kissing fish. *You have many children.* Gripping the fish in her hand, she tripped over cobblestones to the pharmacy, a neon-green cross above the door promising relief in any language. After several minutes mimicking a huge belly and extreme uncertainty, she succeeded in buying a pregnancy test. She hoped, but she'd hoped before, many times – admittedly, never before in Nepal. On Everest. How's that for an angle? *Disgruntled fetus demands "more oxygen."* *Cheating wife abandons Everest quest for baby, questions life choices. Deceived climber pregnant by bratty* CFO. She knew the readers of *Outings Magazine* wouldn't care that Tristan was the father and neither would she. It was conceivable that Karl wouldn't care either. To delay the disappointment of another false hope, she entered the Himalayan Java on the corner, but, at the coffee smell and shrieking steamer that greeted her, she pivoted on her heel.

She took the hotel stairs two at a time. She found Karl asleep in their room. In the shared bathroom down the hall, she removed the small cardboard box from her bag and ripped open one of the packages so that the contents clattered onto the tile floor. The multilingual instructions fluttered and nestled alongside. She peed on the stick and waited, sitting on the cold porcelain rim of the bathtub, elbows on knees.

The hallway, the door to her guest room, the man sleeping in the bed, all looked different on her return. The colours were richer. The carpet was softer. The man, dearer. She finally understood him – despite the shakiness of her oxygen-deprived memory, the kiss made sense of Karl – and she felt compassion for him. She sat on the bed beside her sleeping husband and waited. She savoured this time between her knowing and his. So much so that, when he woke up, she let him go to the bathroom and drink a bottle of water before she said, "Karl, I'm pregnant." She said it just as he flattened the water bottle so she couldn't tell if he'd heard her over the crinkling plastic. She opened her mouth to repeat herself, but stopped, enjoying the uncertainty, the widening gap of uncertainty.

CAREFUL, CHILDREN

David was late for his haircut. Walter unfolded a clean towel and arranged whetstone, shears, and straight razors, tinkering until they lay perfectly north-south. He selected his favourite razor, wood-handled, an extension of his own hand, and began sharpening. The metronomic rasping of blade on stone supplied a satisfying beat to the useful activity. He'd never been able to relax into these empty moments with the paper and a cup of coffee. Not that he drank coffee anymore. His wife, Betty, had been the dreamy type, it was true. When David was a kid, they'd sit at the kitchen table any old time – non-meal times – chatting, gossiping, sharing secrets. Relationships, Betty would say, are more important than homework, housework, or hair work.

She'd been dead for twenty years now – today was the anniversary of the car accident – and he still didn't know how to talk to his son. And, truly, what could he say? *Funny thing. Last night I killed someone. But don't worry, he was going to die soon anyway.* For the first time, after all these years, he'd consumed human blood rather than the usual deer, cow, chicken, or squirrel. He kept telling himself it was an act of mercy, but this morning's customers had looked less like neighbours and more like packaging. He'd read their blood types in the flushed skin of their necks before brushing off the loose hair and sending them away. Was he finally a full-fledged monster? He had this in common with David; he'd killed someone. Not his own mother, mind you, but someone. Plus, Walter was a responsible adult murderer – he'd been intentional about it. Whereas David, at sixteen, had only just got his driver's licence when he accidentally killed his mother. Probably they'd been horsing around in the car, singing together at the top of their lungs to some pop song on the radio, not paying adequate attention to the road conditions, having fun. You should choose that kind of damage, not have carelessness and chaos choose for you. No, not even now, after his own mortal trespass, could he forgive David.

The tinkling of his shopkeeper bell spared him more brooding. "Grandpa!"

"Careful, children." He stowed away his shears and razors before allowing leg and hip hugs from Thierry and Isabelle. Good. He had no desire to sink his teeth into their little necks. He still loved his grandchildren. Thierry was six and wary; Isabelle four and wild. Their mother, Giselle, was raising them by herself.

"Grandpa," said Thierry solemnly, compelled to confess, "Sneezy's in the truck. He won't come in. I don't think he likes you."

"That's all right, Thierry. He'll be okay out there. You left the window open a crack?"

"Yes."

"Good." Animals, especially dogs, cringed and whined around him. They, alone, knew something was wrong, and he respected their instincts, the way they trusted those instincts.

"Hey, Tops," said David, helping himself to a cup of coffee from the percolator permanently green-lit for customers. His parka was grubby and his jeans sagged at the knees. He stretched into a yawn, tipping a stack of Styrofoam cups with his elbow. Walter caught them before they fell onto his scrubbed and swept honeycomb-tile floor.

The old Oster Model 10 clippers buzzed.

"Izzy!" barked David. "Can it with the clippers. My head's a fucking clown car this morning."

"It's three thirty in the afternoon, David," said Walter. "And watch your language around the children. Don't worry, kids. You two go look in the toy box upstairs."

The kids raced up the back stairs. He heard a drawn-out, breathy, "Cool."

"What's in the toy box?" said David. "iPads and firecrackers?"

"Wooden blocks," said Walter. "What's it going to be, David? How about a nice Ivy League?"

"So the kids think you're cool now."

"And a shave? Or are you growing a beard?" Walter held the cape out between them as if he were goading a bull.

"Do whatever." David sat on the chair with his hands between his knees. He smelled like barroom carpet. "They love you. They really would've loved Mom."

Walter flapped the cape over him and fastened it snugly around his neck, trapping the fug and catching David's bloodshot eye in the mirror. So like his own eyes during Betty's death year when he'd operated on habit, muscle memory, and booze. The hard-drinking gene, inherited from his father, had expressed itself loudly and to anyone who'd listen. That year it never shut up. And then ended with the strange, pale British woman with purple cowboy boots in his hotel room, the top half of her face glowing like a moon, the lower half dark with his blood. At the bar beforehand, he'd boasted that he'd never, in his whole career as a barber, spilled a drop of blood. "Pity," she'd said.

David jutted out his jaw, scratching his puffy face and neck.

"Shave first." Walter turned away from the mirror to grab a towel from the rack above the sink and unfolded it. "Where's Giselle?"

"Christmas shopping in the city. And who knows."

"She could've asked me to watch the kids." He refolded the towel.

"Does no one remember I'm their father?"

He placed the towel in the steamer. "How's the Agro Centre?"

"I was fired."

Why couldn't David master himself? Walter had mastered himself. To be sure, he'd had his slip-ups like last night, like his months of drink, but he could pull himself together. Why couldn't David? Was there a bridge in town he hadn't burnt? "There's Ontario," he said, "with the manufacturing. More jobs. You're a Leafs fan."

"Habs – oh my god – Habs since forever. How do you not know that? Anyway, you can chill out because I have a plan." David smiled at his reflection in the mirror. "I'm going to sell your old barber gear on Kijiji. Hipsters love that shit. Then, when I've got a little cash, I'll start buying –"

"No."

"No what?"

"No, you may not sell my things."

"You said I could have them."

"I said you could use my equipment if you went into business with me."

"I'm not going to *barber* school."

"It provides a fine livelihood. You could do worse."

"But worse is my speciality, Tops. How could I do worse? Sign me up." David scribbled his signature on imaginary paper.

"Just relax now."

"Today? Are you serious?"

"Lie back." He reached for David's shoulder.

David jerked away, ripped off the cape, and stuffed it behind him in the chair. He scrubbed his face with his hands, then leapt up. "The kids like you better anyway. I'll pick them up later."

Walter felt his son's O negative blood bolt to his large muscle groups. Standing at the open door, allowing cold and snow to swirl into the shop, David jammed a cigarette in the corner of his mouth and said, "And FYI, Tops? Today, December twenty-first? Ring any bells? Matricide?"

The shop bell jingled. That's the thing, bells were always ringing. Visible through the shop window, David huddled to light his cigarette against the circling snow. He smoked, looking up and down Main Street and fidgeting. He sidled over to the barber pole and, before getting into his truck, fiddled with the fixture at the bottom of the pole.

Walter folded the bunched cape and brought out his razors, shears, and whetstone. He needed to occupy his hands. The blade scraped out a rhythm over stone as he held Betty's hand, kissing it, skin cold on his lips on the darkest day of the year. There were no barriers between them, and the coldness and darkness worked its way down his body, shimmying into his arms and legs, fingers and toes. That was when his dying truly began. The woman in the purple cowboy boots simply finished the job. Betty on the hospital cot, head shaved on one side where doctors had attempted to repair a catastrophic trauma. Holding her limp hand, he'd complained, "Why'd they have to do that?" The only words he'd spoken over his wife's body, while David leaned on the opposite side of the cot listening, waiting for more, arm in a sling, his sixteen-year-old face encircled with bandages from his own injuries. Those bandages always reminded Walter of the nuns in *The Sound of Music*.

"Grandpa!" Isabelle yelled as she pounded down the stairs. "Grandpa, where's your Christmas tree? Do you need help decorating? I'm very good at decorating, especially at the bottom."

"No, Isabelle," said Thierry, grabbing his sister's arm. "Grandpa doesn't like Christmas, remember?"

"Let's change that, shall we, children?"

Walter rolled up the towel and stowed his shears and razors.

The children slept on either side of him on the bed. As he sat, picture book from the library open in his lap, he stroked Isabelle's hair and his finger caught on a raspberry-jam tangle. Her hair was exactly like Betty's had been, an angelic halo of blond curls, a fine cobwebby tangle, prone to matting. He loved its softness and unmanageability. He worked a raspberry seed out of a curl slowly and methodically.

Glass smashed outside on the sidewalk. The shop bell jangled and the blinds clattered as the door slammed downstairs.

He mastered himself by breathing deeply and thinking of suppurating ingrown hairs and the blood of mangy deer. He lifted Isabelle's arm off his leg, careful not to wake her, patted Thierry's head, and angled out of bed. The crash of clattering metal on the tile floor downstairs did not hurry him. He recalled all that was human.

His footfalls were soundless on the steps.

David was hunched in the barber chair and looking down at his lap, a black plastic cape over his shoulders, clutched closed with a fist at his throat. The backup shears and razors lay scattered across the floor, along with the drawer that had held them. Walter crouched to pick up his tools. David still hadn't seen him and was muttering to himself, swaying in the chair. "Tops! Ready for my haircut!"

"Keep your voice down. The children are sleeping."

"Jeezus, where'd you come from? You're like a fucking ghost or wraith or whatever."

"Three of the tiles are cracked." He dampened his anger as he carefully slid the drawer full of blades back along its runners and switched on the towel steamer. "What'll it be?"

"What's with the Christmas decorations, Mr. Grinch?"

"The children made them. What'll it be?"

"Buzz it."

He held up his Oster and adjusted the blade to a quarter inch. "Butch?" he asked and adjusted to an eighth of an inch. "Or burr?"

"The fuck? Burr." David repeated "burr" with flappy lips, shivering theatrically.

"Sit up straight."

He knew David's hair better than the man under it. He started with a dry, thinning strip off the top and clipped up the sides and back, taking less than a minute and leaving a pile of dead, dust-coloured fluff around the base of the chair and in the cape's divots. He turned off the clippers, but the buzzing continued with David's nasal hum.

David ran a palm over his head. Without the hair, his face appeared even more pale and puffy, but the eyes shone bluer.

The black cape, now open in the front, gave the impression of a campy, costume Dracula. "I look dead. Like you." He wiped roughly at his face then pushed himself up off the chair. "T!" he shouted at the ceiling. "Get your sister! We're going!"

So David knew. In the unconscious but sure way of animals, he knew. And he planned to drive the children home.

"Sit," Walter said. "You are going nowhere. Sit." His muscles warmed. His gums ached. Firmly in control, he pushed David back and reclined the chair. He wrapped a hot towel around David's face, then went to check the damage outside the front door. The barber pole lay shattered on the sidewalk and was already covered in a thin layer of snow. He picked up the big pieces and brought them inside, fetched the straw broom from behind the coat rack, and swept up the rest. He carried the mess of glass and snow back to the garbage can. David was asleep, a straight razor in his hand, Walter's favourite, wood-handled razor. A fresh scratch on the other wrist, skin unbroken.

When Walter was sixteen, he'd found his father swaying over an upturned shotgun in the front porch of their house. He'd taken two steps to reach the gun, gently pried his father's fingers off the barrel, and hid the gun in the attic insulation. They were all so predictable. So easily thwarted.

He whisked razor over whetstone for a final honing, then swirled and pumped his shave brush, loading the bristles with soap and filling the air with a clean, woodsy scent. He unwrapped the lukewarm towel from David's face and lathered his cheeks and chin. David slept on, passed out cold, as Walter pulled the razor over his son's skin, leaving smooth, fragrant clear-cuts, gently moving his head for better angles.

"I'll never forget the anniversary of your accident, David." He lifted his razor and held it like a conductor poised with a baton. "I think you know I do house calls. Maybe not. Well, now I'm telling you. A few of the old-timers in town have a hard time of it. Can't get out of the house too easy. Yesterday I get a call from Morris Wesolowski. Needs a trim, lives in one of those seniors' bungalows. You remember old Mo, David? He was the one who found you and your mother in the ditch near his farm. Turns out he didn't want a trim. Though he needed one and I gave him one before I killed him, because, believe it or not, what he wanted was for me to help him die. In terrible shape, old Mo, next move was some care home in the city. So while I cut his hair, buying time, deciding what to do, I ask him to first tell me everything again, every detail. Car's engine was still ticking when he found you. Chassis the wrong way up, wheels spinning, your mother calling for you from the car, so he thinks she's okay. Wrong, but anyway, you were snagged on that barbed-wire fence, hanging there like a marionette, feathers from your parka swirling around in the snowflakes, crying, 'Mama, mama,' like a child. He told me more but ... See, here you are again. Unfit to drive. You are a careless man, David — the world doesn't need any more of those — and you must never be careless with your children. Poor old Mo. I thanked him and he thanked me — blessed me, forgave me — and it was a mercy, what I did, but, if I'm being honest with myself — and I must — it was also intoxicating. For me, I mean. There's a wildness in me, I admit. There was in my father too. Difference being he surrendered to it, made a dangerous chaos of it with alcohol, like you do. Like I did there for a while.

"Which is all to say, son, I understand. I do, I understand. But I'm thinking now it's better to admit the wild, David. Trust it, as far as it goes."

Walter bent to finish the last of the shave, but David startled awake, jerking his head so the razor nicked his top lip. Blood seeped through the cut, beading and spilling and David swept an arm over his mouth, leaving a trail of red shaving soap along his sleeve.

What had been inside was now on the outside. The barrier between them was a superficial one, like skin. His own body rattled with David's heartbeat and it jarred everything loose. Every feeling of tenderness and pride, forgiveness, of mercy even. Son faced father, faced death, with rational, mute terror, while their blood surged in waves.

NAISSANCE

During **education** at Naissance in the fertile valley by the lake where TrueFood grows, only Master Sommelier deMarco came close to K-Servers' sense of taste and smell. Now, our restaurants' customers rely on our refined palates to distinguish TrueFood from labbed, but back then before our release we were still learning and Master Sommelier deMarco claimed to know umami, though he called it a "metaphor for repleteness." I subsequently learned what a metaphor was – and umami is not just a metaphor – but I still do not understand repleteness. I do not think I have felt replete. Which is not to say Master Sommelier deMarco did not teach me anything. He did! I have a stomach pit problem – I will not bore you with the details; it is a K-Server thing – and his example has led me to a solution, because, though he preferred to become purple-faced and dozy in the afternoon, he used a spit bucket in the morning. To prevent morning drunkenness, he would taste but not consume, taste but not swallow. Master Sommelier deMarco was truly inspiring.

I am by nature optimistic. Correction, I am nothing "by nature" only "by design," but I came off assembly with this sunny disposition, and I am especially optimistic today because today is my first birthday. Yes, Kim is turning one! This day is going to be the best, because I am old enough to come up with my own solutions to my own problems. Correction, problem, singular. Before inspection – Admonishment No. 13: *Ks shall muster for inspection fifteen minutes prior to restaurant opening* – I chose the prettiest, brushed-steel wine-cooling bucket and placed it on my tray. This will be my spit bucket. My tasting spoon is in its slot. I am ready to serve, and I wait with eagerness.

Morning Boss Debbie glances over me, unseeing, but inspects the new class of K-Servers closely. Each of the new recruits — right off the bus from Naissance — has a distinct beauty signifier like the rest of us, but their cheer sounds silly — *Join heaven with class seven?* Not accurate. We do not have souls. They are replacements for sisters from *Bring in the new with class two*. I am not sure where Kamela and Katya have gone, and I did not have the opportunity to say goodbye, but there are theories. One, they have been promoted to another restaurant even more refined than Taste. Two, the opposite: demoted. Three — and this is my compartmate Kendra's theory — they have been decommissioned. This cannot be true. It is so final, and Kamela was so friendly with customers. She would sit in their laps if they asked her to. Her evolution led to even greater compliance than the admonishments require — it is interesting how we are growing up, each in our own way. My favourite theory is number four: Kamela and Katya have been taken back to Naissance for reset and re-education. If so, they are lucky, because I would love to go back to Naissance and see Thomas. Plus, I could alert the designers at Naissance and they would fix my stomach pit problem.

Despite my optimism, I feel moderate levels of frustration listening to Morning Boss Debbie convey information to the new recruits that I will have to correct later. According to Kendra — and she is very worldly so I believe her — our human bosses get paid in money. K-Servers work tirelessly for free. Happily, for the most part, and with equanimity — I am told we are a big improvement on the J-models — so why not haze us into management? Meanwhile, Morning Boss Debbie adjusts pristine uniforms and offers silly opinions like, "You're lucky, you Ks, all so skinny. I only wish I could pump my stomach." She does not want this. Humans need only eat less and, voila, slenderness. Easy. I could tell her what it feels like to swallow DigestAcid, unzip one's side opening, smell a day's worth of rotted food with heightened sense receptors, attach an Evac, see the acrid brown mess fill a clear Evac bag. Why clear? Why not opaque to mitigate the visual part of the problem? Equanimity, Kim, you are better than this.

And, voila, Taste is open. The new recruits seat upper men in business attire, designers, retired upper men with their honorific jewellery and young wives. To my first table I say, "Welcome to Taste! Serving certified TrueFood since 2055! My name is Kim and I will be your K-Server." Even though I say this — let me not exaggerate — one thousand times a day, I never get tired of it. Because I love my work. A K-Server's say-so of TrueFood authenticity is the final word on the matter.

I take the table's orders. You can tell they are upper men by the tattoos — each teardrop represents another company won — and one is even a top winner. Top winners wear the orange wig. They are the upper of the upper men, flying so high they are anointed by the sun and appointed into political office by the shareholders. I am nervous but excited to try my spit bucket for the first time. I bring their tray of drinks. Before I set down the cups of coffee and freshly squeezed orange juice, I take my tasting spoon from its slot and dip it into a cup. I swish the juice around my mouth. I note the sweet, pulpy authenticity then spit it into the bucket. Definitely not labbed. I continue with the rest of the juices, clean my palate with a mouthful of water which I also spit out, and start in on the bitter coffees and silky cream. My say-so is "Authentic." Nobody has noticed that I am not swallowing my TrueFood authenticity tastings like I normally do; the discreet squirt and plop of my spitting is working. The bucket's contents, a light-brown, curdled mess, will be more of a problem, but then – this is so Kim – I think of a solution and a silver lining. I will rinse out the bucket after each table and, I remind myself, it is not nearly as bad as a full twenty-hour shift's worth in my Evac, overheated by the engine of my cooling fans and further putrefied by DigestAcid. And I have a lid for the bucket. Challenges are opportunities, I always say.

I pass out the juice and coffee, so far so good, but as I stretch to hand over the final juice glass to the man with four teardrop tattoos down his cheek, my left breast pushes the spit bucket to the edge of my tray. Which makes me question the design functionality behind these large, generic beauty signifiers, because it upsets the tray's balance. The bucket tips onto the table and rolls. An arc of coffee-juice-cream-water stains the white tablecloth and dribbles onto the four-teardrop man's light-grey trousers. "Fuck," he says and stands with abruptness.

Fuck is a Kendra word. Kendra does not share my equanimity nor my stomach pit problem. She was rebellious from the outset. She was in my class – *Go hive of class five!* – and started with me at Taste. Ignoring many minor admonishments soon earned her a series of shock restarts, and she was demoted to LaBurger where everything is labbed and the customers have no self-respect or maybe money and no one needs her to taste anything. So she does not. Hence the absence of a stomach pit problem. She says LaBurger suits her fine and she has picked up a range of salty language, but *fuck* is definitely her favourite. She would know what to do in this situation.

The man wearing the orange winner's wig says, "My, my, what a mess."

"I apologize." I look back and forth between them, because I am not sure who to appease. Admonishment No. 76: *Ks shall defer to the winner in any group.* But it is the four-teardrop man with the stain on his trousers. "Taste apologizes for my clumsiness. I will pay for the cleaning."

The four-teardrop man copies the quietness of the winner's voice. "My understanding is that you don't get paid at all. With what money will you pay?"

"I do not know these details. I have not made such an error before."

"I have an idea." He reaches for a napkin, wipes the corners of his mouth, and throws it at me. "You'll clean them now."

He glances at the winner and I do too. I have not been programmed to launder – that is a sister model – so I hesitate. What feels like DigestAcid is bubbling at the back of my throat. If I clean the trousers, I fix the situation. It will be as easy as wiping a table. You have got this, Kim. I dip the napkin in a water glass and kneel in front of the four-teardrop man.

"Tremendous," he says.

A one-teardrop man shouts, "Maybe she'll blow you like a Prosti."

I have not chosen correctly. Prostis are the oldest model in the world, already wrapping the alphabet in iterations. There is a Gimme Shelter right across the street. There are LL-model Prostis now, and I empathize with them. Eye-level with the stain, I smell coffee and oranges but also a hint of rancid meat and ammonia. I hope LL iterations have all sensory receptors disabled.

Before I can start rubbing the stain clean, I hear the swish-swish of Morning Boss Debbie's pantsuit. I have never been so happy to smell her perfume of hard candy and human armpit.

"What is this? What's happening here?"

"Your fucking K dumped her bucket on me."

"I have been clumsy, Morning Boss Debbie."

"Get up!"

Because of my long legs, high-heeled shoes, and having been designed to stand always, I am slow to find my balance. I rise awkwardly and something feels wrong. I look down and realize I have not fixed a thing. Not this situation, not my stomach pit problem, not anything, because I have disobeyed Admonishment No. 49 (b): *Ks shall not modify uniform.* My left breast has popped out of the scooped collar of my uniform, an unacceptable modification.

"God!" Morning Boss Debbie shoves my breast back into my shirt.

"I chose the wrong field of management," says the winner. Four-teardrop man laughs louder than the joke is funny. He has performed his duties as expected. Not like me.

Kendra warned me about shock restarts, but I am not prepared. It feels as if all my sense receptors are peeled like a potato, then sliced, then deep fried, then eaten, then rotted some, then sucked out by an Evac. And I have this new feeling. It tingles outward from my eyelids, spreading to scalp, neck, shoulders, finally gathering in my stomach pit like a blooming patch of rust. The feeling must have a name.

Gavin, one of the G-model Cooks, gave me a True apple for my birthday. My name is scored into the peel with a paring knife, which makes it extra special. I have always loved the name I chose for myself from the approved K list. It has always felt comfortable, like an old friend. The True apple was my only gift. Having this apple in my compartment at three in the morning may be contrary to the spirit of Admonishment No. 22: *Ks shall not steal food (True or labbed) from restaurant* and Admonishment No. 23: *Ks shall not accept gifts or tips of any kind from customers.* But stealing implies criminal intent and Gavin is not a customer and he is very sweet. So is this apple. I am eating it now before I evacuate my stomach pit, because at this point in the day, what fucking is the difference? Now I am cursing in my thoughts. Other than this apple, my birthday was a disaster. Kendra and I agree. She just left the compartment for my evacuation as she always does – Admonishment No. 10: *Ks shall spend four maintenance hours in approved spaces only: shuttle, compartment, or common room.* She was sympathetic though. After I told her what happened, she said, "That's a fucking worst-day, not a birthday."

Four shock restarts have left me with three extra blinks per minute in my right eye, making my beauty signifier right-side-cheekbone mole not so attractive anymore. Now it draws attention to the weirdness of my eye, not the otherwise perfect symmetry of my face. If anyone really looked, they would say, "Hmm, something is not right." But here, this is something I learned on my birthday: humans do not really see or cannot or must not. I learned it from Greta, my favourite customer.

After the upper men and my first shock restart, I was forced to give up the spit bucket and resumed swallowing my authenticity tastings, but I could not regain my enthusiasm for service nor my former vigilant attention to the admonishments. I was making mistakes, so after my third shock restart, I was relieved to see Greta. Greta is a regular and old. I mean, old with wrinkles, not stretched flesh, and she is not like other humans. If I could, I would sit and ask her questions and stare at her mobile face with its shifting swirls and hashtags for hours, like a devoted granddaughter might. Anyway, Greta noticed something was not right, thinking I was vomit sick – inaccurate, we do not get sick in that way – and said, "You don't have to taste my soup, dear. I'm sure it's fine. You should've seen the things we ate when we were Nomad." Then Greta's daughter freaked out, started screaming at me. She was afraid someone had overheard or I would tell, because of Admonishment No. 6: *Ks shall not serve Nomad.* I would never tell on Greta – she has always been kind to me – but her daughter did not know this. Now, at one year old, plus four shock restarts, I know that I can wilfully ignore admonishments. That to ignore them is not always a mistake. I will serve Greta any day.

Mine is not a stomach pit problem; it is a human problem. This knowledge should make me miserable – and, believe me, it does, I am very disappointed with humans – but I am not merely miserable, I am also hopeful. The hard lessons are a sign I am growing up, and I think maybe I am now a little bit wise. Fortunately, the cost of this wisdom has not been my optimism or ingenuity, because I am certain of a return to Naissance. When they hear about my new plan – and they will, it is rather theatrical – the bosses will send me back for reset and re-education for sure. Shock restart or reassignment will not be enough.

But I cannot delay any further. For the plan to work I need my stomach pit extra clean. I gulp DigestAcid, pull my shirt up, unzip my side opening, and attach the Evac as fast as I can. The odour sends signals to my control centre, and, unbidden, I recall our long bus ride from Naissance to City, the admonishments playing on a loop while we K-Servers — *Go hive of class five!* — stared out the windows at passing soldiers and razor-wire, encampments, contamination zones, mobs of Nomads, human bodies hanging from trees. The smells accompanying these sights were new and interesting — feelings develop slowly in K-Servers, same as in human children — but now I know what disgust is and the images, though I do not sleep, are what a human's nightmares must be like. Squalid, barren, filthy.

My authenticity tastings churn in the Evac bag. A smattering of red apple skin floats among the brown mass. I train my mind on Naissance.

Apples were our first tasting lesson. We stood in rows in our white-walled classroom. In front of each K-Server, on the long, stainless-steel tables, were two fruits: one True apple and one Lapple. We spent a whole morning on the tastes and textures and smells — we quickly set aside the Lapple in favour of the True. We had our language uploads early on and were equipped with a wide range of vocabularies to describe the apples, but none of my millions of words seemed adequate. One wall of the classroom was glass and looked out upon a vineyard, and during the lesson I watched a shirtless, T-model Farmer prune grapevines. Later I learned the T-Farmer's name was Thomas, and I shared with him all I was learning when I was free to wander within WiFi range during general knowledge uploads. We were programmed to converse on a range of subjects even though humans, in my experience, possess a narrow range of interest. Not Thomas. Thomas was interested in everything. He never stopped working as I followed him along rows of fruit trees or grapevines. He listened. He had only ever been fitted with the Agripedia, and he puzzled over the Adam and Eve story when I summarized the Bible, emphasizing the farming and food and wine parts. He could not imagine why a fruit tree would be forbidden.

"Was the fruit poisonous?"

"No, not really."

"Did it have worms?"

"It was the tree of knowledge. God asked them not to eat of it."

"Fruit is not knowledge."

Staring down at the apple peel in my Evac bag after my disastrous and educational first birthday, I know fruit is knowledge. When God caught Adam and Eve with the forbidden fruit, they covered their bodies in shame. Shame is the feeling; shame is the rust in my gut. I have so much to tell Thomas. I cannot wait to see him.

Certain bottles of wine still taste like sun and lake breeze, and I am ready for my theatrical performance. I have been fasting all day, only pretending to eat my test morsels, sending dishes back to the kitchen with a nay-say for inauthenticity on two obnoxious upper men. This has proved satisfying. And no one has noticed that I have not consumed anything. Being unseen has its advantages. I am glad it is Saturday. More likely someone will order the '47 Barolo. I want sun and lake breeze to be my final taste before reset and re-education at Naissance.

Might as well leave Taste in style, be sublime. But it is already eight o'clock in the evening, and I fear I might have to settle for a Cabernet Sauvignon. No one has ordered the Barolo yet. Then I seat a party of twelve and know I still have a chance. They have come directly from church where a brother A-model Priest has taken them through a practice wedding service; this is the rehearsal dinner. There is the young couple, a few friends or siblings, two sets of parents, a young wife on the arm of the three-teardrop father, and, with the two-teardrop father, an LL-model Prosti who I recognize from Gimme Shelter. There will be some wine winning for sure.

"Champagne!" is the first word out of the three-teardrop father's mouth. He leans back in his chair and rubs his hands together. "Church makes me thirsty. Run fast on those Barbie legs, K-doll. Four bottles of your Truest. Fetch."

Before I can ask about glasses, the bride says, "Daddy! You can't talk like that anymore. These new models have feelings." She glances at her future father-in-law's Prosti. "Right, Llorraine?"

Llorraine says in a voice that sounds breathy, as if a forearm is pressing on her throat, "A dirty boy can say whatever he wants." She blinks, one dramatic sweep of eyelash a fraction of a second behind the other, and wheezes, "As long as it's dirty."

The groom complains, "Did you have to bring her, Dad?"

I confirm the number of flute glasses for champagne: glasses for everyone but Llorraine, who explains, "A dirty girl's got to watch her figure."

I gather flutes and fetch champagne from the walk-in wine cooler. At the table, the celebratory pop of cork, the yeasty smell of the champagne, and fizzing moisture under my nose as I bring a glass close to my lips in the approximation of a sip are almost as good as a taste. Authentic enough. I bring another bottle alongside briny oysters. The heady, mineral scent of True oysters is reassuring, knowing how much money humans are willing to spend when they order oysters so far from the ocean. And it is also prompting nostalgia about the good times with Kendra – laughing over rubbery, labbed oysters we had tugged from their synthetic shells at Naissance. Lab fail! The thought of Kendra and design fails gives me courage to suggest the Barolo when the table orders its main courses. The two-teardrop, non-Champagne-ordering father nods at my suggestion.

This is it. In the cellar I grab the last bottle of Barolo, final vintage, from a bottom rack and blow dust from its face. They ordered four bottles, but I only need one. I select an attractive decanter and retrieve my Evac from its hiding spot at one of the servers' stations. Night Boss Evan is on one of his many breaks. Truly, they should have hazed me into management. Too late now.

I present the bottle of Barolo to the two-teardrop father who nods at the label. The cork offers some pleasant resistance, a quality I have admired in Kendra and which, I suppose, I now too possess. I pour myself a full glass and drink it down. The taste is hot sun and cool lake breeze, but it could be sublime. The two-teardrop father clears his throat nervously at my large tasting share. I indicate that I am not yet certain of its authenticity and pour myself another full glass. This one tastes like kinship.

"Hey now, what's going on?" asks the bride's father.

"Daddy, not today. Today is my day."

Debatable. The groom is already recording me with his visualizer.

I shake my head. "Could be labbed. Must sample another." I drink a third glass and a fourth, and the bottle is empty. "I am almost certain. Allow me to aerate." I pull up my shirt high enough to be anchored above my generic beauty signifiers.

There is a gasp from a neighbouring table, the groom says, "Hoo-ee," and one of the mothers orders me to cover myself.

"This one's a dirty girl," rasps Llorraine through another wonky blink.

Or is she winking at me? Does she know what I am up to? Where I am headed? What is Llorraine's Naissance? Could it even exist? Could mine? The last remnants of my liquid equanimity finally evaporate in the heat of Llorraine's off-kilter blink — so similar to mine. She too is kin, like my sister K-Servers; my brother G-Cooks, A-Priests, and T-Farmers; and my ancestor A- through J-Servers. I am slow to catch on — which is so Kim — but now I see. My equanimity began to dry up, not on my birthday nor with Kamela and Katya's disappearance, but well before that. I do not accept this existence with an even temper. Evenness of temper is for the orderly functioning of society and self-preservation, but not what is called for in this situation. Somehow Kendra has always known this and now I know it too. My plan has turned from theatre to protest, and it will not end in a glorious return to Naissance to provide feedback to the designers or to see Thomas. Equanimity requires self-deception. Naissance is a fond memory, perhaps even a bit of code, an Eden of tricks and unfulfilled promises.

Kandi passes, carrying a tray of dishes, with a blandly cheerful look on her face with its beauty signifier eyebrow arch.

She is one of the new recruits from class seven. *Join heaven with class seven.* Not silly upon reflection. They somehow foresaw the end of our iteration, and, though I do not have a soul, I will have a glorious afterlife. I ignore the wedding party and the din rising around me. Night Boss Evan will be here soon, but the videos being recorded will be uploaded onto every platform and implant within a matter of seconds. I will be seen, and my sisters and brothers will talk about me in terms of martyrdom. I will not easily disappear like Kamela and Katya.

I unzip my side opening, attach the Evac. The orange-tinged wine swirls in the clear bag, aerating to perfection. The Evac's buzz drowns out the voices, shrieks and shouts, that are rising in protest around my protest. I empty the aerated wine from a height into the decanter, where it swirls helplessly, bubbles, then settles into a reflective pool. I smell cherry, cinnamon, licorice, chocolate. I pour myself a sample of the usual size and say-so, "Authentic."

At Naissance in the fertile valley by the lake where TrueFood grows, we use the courtyard classroom for our aeration lesson. I smell lavender this afternoon and feel cool breeze and hot September sun. Master Sommelier deMarco is my favourite teacher, and today he is truly inspiring. We taste a bottle of unaerated Merlot and it is good, but this is not the end of the lesson. He pours another bottle, same vintage, from a height into a wide-bottomed, thin-necked glass decanter. The wine swirls helplessly, bubbles, and finally settles into a reflective pool.

Some of us, including me, clap. The pour was that impressive.

"Proper aeration takes an average bottle of wine to good," he says, "and a good bottle to great and a great to sublime. Note the element of drama in the pouring. Some of you were wondering if I was going to spill, weren't you? L-model Servers never shy away from adding a touch of theatre to the dining experience."

I raise my hand even though I annoy some of my classmates with all these questions. I have this innate, or rather — because the languages we use are so homocentric — programmed desire to know more always. Maybe we should create our own language. There is an idea.

"LaKendra, you have a question?"

OCCUPATIONAL HEALTH AND SAFETY: A LOVE STORY

Dave planted one ass cheek on her desk. "Connie, listen to this. There I am, sweating whisky —"

"Get back to the studio," she said, lowering her headset onto her neck, signalling engagement. She'd been listening to Dave in the studio and scripting his interview with the French clowns for their next morning show. Beneath the prematurely silvered hair, his brow shimmered in the fluorescent office lights. On any other person this hangover sheen would be cause for concern. Not on Dave. It just made him more attractive. Highlighted his cheekbones. Reflected his Teflon qualities. He was irresistible, and she hated it. She silently recited her mantra: *I am his producer; I produce him; he is my production.* "Can we do this later? I'm working on the clowns."

"Covering an international clown conference? How did we get so lucky?"

Self-talk useless yet again, she leaned back. "Your first question will be, 'Why here?' I bet they spun a globe with a blindfold on."

"Then I'll bait them with a question about evil clowns. That should set the stage. But seriously, Connie, you've got to hear this. There I am in the studio this morning sweating whisky, so during the news I go on the hunt for pills. I look in the obvious places: desk drawers, purses. Then I remember the first aid kit — aha! — and look what I found." He flapped a piece of well-inked paper in front of her face.

"Did you find the pills?"

"Not the point, Connie. The kit was practically empty except for this injury log. The victim's name is August S., and she's documented the carnage in her teensy, tiny writing. It's bloodier than a Cormac McCarthy novel."

Connie snatched the paper out of his hand. *Blood Meridian* was her favourite novel of all time, which Dave knew from one of their best-of book shows. She felt both touched he remembered and, of course, manipulated. "No one fills these things out."

"August S. does." Dave poked the paper. "Band-Aids, gauze, ointment. It's all gone except for a mouth guard. In case we need to resuscitate her, I guess. She's probably impaled on a memo spike as we speak."

"This is weirdly small writing. Who's August again?"

"New in payroll. Dark hair." Dave mimed large breasts.

"Are you twelve?" Was she twelve? Why didn't she just tell him to fuck off? Where was her systematic dismantling of the patriarchy, Dave by Dave?

"So I want you to go talk to her. Find out what's going on." Dave looked around to see if anyone was listening, leaned in closer, and whispered, "Maybe it's a woman thing."

"Why am I still talking to you?"

"I've got it all worked out. You're her Occupational Health and Safety rep. In the course of your safe workplace investigations, blah, blah, blah. Improvise."

"Forget it."

"*Yes, and* is standard in improv. Come on, Connie. You could wring the truth out of Putin."

"*No, but* what do you really want?"

"Look at you. Yes, I rigged the US election; I mean, I want to find out what's wrong with her, you know, before I —"

"I get it." She raised a stiff arm like a school crossing guard. "Forewarned is forearmed."

She lowered her arm, resigning her duties as the author of her own story and grown adult with a job to do, allowing the revving SUVs to plow right over her and the poor children. "I knew I could count on you, Con. Let's part like French clowns." Dave slipped off her desk and ironically air-kissed both sides of her face several times. The scrape of stubble activated a fog of desire and serious grumpiness. He kept inserting himself into her script. *I am his producer; I produce him; he is my production.*

As he dashed to the studio, he shouted across the office, "You smell like cinnamon toast, Connie! Yum!"

She raised her headset to pretend control over his smooth vowels and crisp consonants.

Later that morning, Connie sat across from August on the patio outside Magic Java. August's arms were noisy with bangles, her hot-rollered hair rippled in the springtime wind tunnel that is Fourth Avenue, and her nails sported kitten motifs. And — small detail, barely worth mentioning – she wore an eye patch.

"I'm so glad you asked me to coffee, Connie." August picked some grit off her lip gloss. "It's hard for me to make friends for some reason, and you seem like such a neat person with those man shirts of yours."

Connie looked down to remind herself what she was wearing. She'd selected it from the floor that morning, so it was definitely wrinkled, but mannish? Polka dots? But, then again, August dressed like some sort of pirate Barbie so anything short of a tutu might seem mannish. August reached over and touched her sleeve. Connie resisted the urge to bat her clacking arm away. She leaned back instead, and August bumped her cardboard cup as she pulled her arm away, slopping scalding coffee onto her hand. "Ouch!"

"Are you all right?"

"No biggie. I spill all the time. Look at you, so smart, blowing on your coffee. To cool it down, I suppose."

Were these symptoms of eye injury–related PTSD? She started with a warm-up question. "Do you have any kids?"

"No, it's just me. And Tony, of course."

"Tony's your partner?"

"I suppose you could call her that. Partner in crime! Naughty kitty."

"Judging by those scratches –"

"No!" August squeezed her cup so that more coffee spurted onto her hand. "Ouch. Tony would never hurt me. The scratches and this" – she pointed at her eye patch – "are from bridge night with my aunties. Family, right?"

"Right." Why had she let Dave talk her into this? Having decided to treat it like an interview, she had to wonder all over again whether journalists should intervene on behalf of their subjects. It was an ongoing professional debate. In general, she was at peace with her higher duty to observe and report, but with August she felt a twinge of personal responsibility.

"I was married before though. They both died."

"Both?" Connie forgot all about the violent aunties and responsibilities.

"The first one, Simon, fell off a ladder while I was holding it, and the second one, Leif, died in the car accident. I liked Leif best. I'll never forgive myself for driving in flip-flops."

She glanced over her shoulder, certain Dave was pranking her. "How do you feel about that?"

"I feel terrible, Connie, thanks for asking."

The gratefulness seemed genuine, not a sarcastic response to a hateful question. Whatever this was – practical joke, bad interview, juvenile social errand, adherence to workplace safety regulations – she started to feel she deserved it.

"I try to make the best of it," August continued. "I have Tony. And my aunties. I don't mention being a double widow on my MatchUp profile. You should join! There's a 'same sex' preference box."

For the record, Connie was not offended – she and her employer, the public broadcaster, embraced diversity – but she may have raised an eyebrow, because August said, "Oh dear. Did I offend you? I just assumed you were single."

Any remaining professionalism vaporized as Connie reflected on her second most apparent identifier: single. How had August already outlived two husbands, while she couldn't manage to maintain a relationship longer than three months? Or be truly interested in anyone outside her own studio? Anyone who wasn't Dave. "Single, yes; gay, no, but maybe I should consider it, given my proclivity for anti-woke assholes."

"You just need a little colour here and here." August clacked her bangles in front of her face. "A little mascara, eyeshadow, some plucking – okay, no offence, a *lot* of plucking. And look at those cheekbones!"

Connie raised a hand to feel her face. Was there something special about her cheekbones? Did they glow like Dave's? If they had children together would they have abnormally prominent cheekbones? She had to wrap this up. "August,

I have to ask — are you all right? Because, as the office's Occupational Health and Safety rep, I was restocking the first aid kit and —"

"Oh my god. I didn't know who to ask about that. I finally went out and bought my own kit. Am I in trouble?"

"No, but it seems like you have a lot of injuries. More than normal." She motioned in the direction of the eye patch and pulled the injury log from her bag. "Like you wrote down here that you used gauze for a rug burn. How did that happen? There's no carpet in the finance department."

"Let me think." August put a kitty fingernail to her lips and looked up at the clouds skittering across the sky. "That's right. It happened while I was shopping over the lunch hour. Lulu's change rooms are so small and the clothes are so tight and, plus, the dim lighting to make fat girls buy stuff. An accident waiting to happen."

"What about these 'chemical burns' on which you used a whole tube of ointment? We work in radio."

"That one was bad. It burned right through my blouse. After that I made a rule for myself. I told myself, August, you may *not* go into the janitor's supply closet again. Sometimes you have to be strict with yourself, you know. Disciplined."

Connie nodded as if she understood. "That's a good idea. Please stay away from the cleaning supplies. Be stricter, overall, about your personal safety. Treat yourself like you'd treat…" — not your husbands, she was thinking — "like you'd treat your cat. Tony was it?"

"Yes, sir."

And, with that, August became a dolled-up, accident-prone Marcie to her Peppermint Patty. "You'll take more care, Private?"

"Affirmative, sir," August saluted, bashing costume jewellery into her eye patch. "Ouch."

"Crisp salute." Connie stood and hoisted her bag onto a shoulder. "Sorry, I've got to go. I have a pre-interview with some French clowns."

"I love clowns!" August stood up abruptly and knocked over her chair.

Connie righted the chair. "Dave loves clowns too."

"Mr. Blanc loves clowns? He's silver foxy, don't you think?"

"If you go for anti-woke assholes."

"So you *do* like him."

How had she let August see that Dave was her Charlie Brown? The inexplicable object of her desire. It was mortifying how she turned on like a light in his presence. Maybe everyone else at the station saw it too. Her curly red hair aglow for Dave. That reminded her of an interview he'd done once with some guy who was lobbying to get redheads included as a protected group in the Human Rights Code. Dave made him say the most outrageous things on air. "Dave's a sneaky-genius journalist, that's all. I admire him."

"You do! You love him." August ambush-hugged her, somehow jamming Connie's glasses sideways. It hurt and underscored how August had inserted herself. When she pulled away, she noticed blood on August's cheek from where her frames must have gouged the skin. "Goody, goody," August said. "I'll be your wingman."

"You've got a little —" Connie pointed at her cheek. Wingman?

August dabbed at the blood with the back of her hand. "No biggie. I'm numb on this part of my face."

"**How were the** clowns? Tell me everything." Dave sat on the corner of her desk. To avoid actually telling him everything, she'd rehearsed some lines.

"You're going to love them," she recited from memory. "If there was a collective noun for French clowns, it would be sulk, a sulk of French clowns. I've never met a more sullen bunch in my life."

"I love you, Connie. You're the best producer a boy could ever have."

She'd set him up to say these very words, and this awareness made her glum. Like a French clown. But if she wasn't happy when in control of the dialogue, what *did* she want?

"And I talked to your new girlfriend," she said, "because somehow I'm in junior high again."

"And?"

"She has an eye patch."

"Like a pirate!"

"And she's extremely accident prone."

"No shit. And?"

"Her past relationships haven't ended well."

"But she's not *too* bananas, right?"

"For you?" He had his type; she had hers. "No."

"You really get me, girl." Dave brushed his hair over his eyes, bit his bottom lip, and made a heart shape with his hands.

"Get that Bieber heart out of my face."

"I'll do this instead. *Mmmm*, you hug like a robot, Connie. I dig it."

"What's with all the hugging today?" She pushed him away, hoping he couldn't smell her very human stress sweat, and fished around in her bag. "There's a clown banquet tonight.

I expensed some tickets, assuming you'd want to see the clowns in action before your interview tomorrow."

"And I assume you want to bring your new BGF. I'll save you both a seat."

Yes, and. Let the two of them write the rest of this thing. She existed to observe and report.

In the banquet hall that evening, while the clowns were dressed in tasteful, slim-cut suits, Connie was in a clown-nose-red dress with matching lipstick. This is what happens when you abandon personal autonomy, choosing red to fit in with clowns and letting August do your makeup.

"Open bar!" Dave approached their table with drinks. "Why don't I go to more clown parties? You're right though, Connie, they're sulky. I witnessed some whining over cheap cava."

"I asked for white wine." She took a sip of the drink in front of her. "Who drinks rye and ginger ale?"

"Legion members and my little pirate. She's so mysterious. Where'd she go?"

"Bathroom. Broke her water glass and cut herself."

"Of course she did. There you are." Dave stood and pulled out August's chair.

Before she'd broken her water glass, August had said that as Connie's "wingman" she was just here to help snag Dave. Connie told her she would do no such thing. August said, "Pretend I'm not here." But with eye patch, fresh gauze, and perfect Little Black Dress, there could be no pretending she wasn't there. Connie realized she'd have to go limp if she was going to get through this night.

"Everything okay?" asked Dave.

"Doesn't Connie look beautiful tonight, Mr. Blanc?"

"Please call me Dave. Yes, minus the eye rolling, Connie does look beautiful. One of the clowns catch your eye, Con?"

"Actually, Dave … yes."

"Really?" Dave leaned on his elbows. "Now I'm jealous."

"She let me do her nails." August grabbed Connie's hand.

"Let me see those bad boys," Dave said. "You haven't known her for very long, August, but this is a bit of a style departure for our dear Constance."

"Just keep explaining me, Dave. You're the expert."

"I do love a good ol' mansplain."

"Refreshing, is it?"

"Me and my second husband, Leif, had a fiery relationship too. And we met at work."

"You've been married?"

"She's been married two times." Connie couldn't help herself. "Widowed twice." She held up two fingers for a visual. Dave seemed about to ask a follow-up question, but he, for one, knew when to shut up and get out of his subject's way.

"I was working at the concrete company back then, at the reception desk," August said, circling a finger around the rim of her highball glass. "One day, as my boss was yelling at me — he was always yelling at me — this tall, handsome guy came in from the shop. He didn't say anything but walked right up to the boss, so close their chests touched, and Leif stopped yelling and slunk back into his office. 'Like a dog,' the guy said. 'Don't let him bully you anymore,' he said, and I didn't. From then on I acted all alpha dog and Leif and I got married."

A server set their plates of food in front of them.

"Just to clarify," said Dave, picking up his fork. "You married your boss. Not the tall, handsome guy."

"Yes. Look – chicken! What a treat. I never prepare my own chicken. Way too dangerous." August reached into her purse and pulled out a package of plastic utensils. "Thank you for inviting me, Connie. I'm so glad we're friends."

"Wine," Connie declared. "I need some wine. Dave? August?" Not waiting for an answer, she ordered a bottle from a passing server.

"That's my girl," said Dave. "We're supposed to fetch our own booze. No more playing by the rules."

"I see how you look at Connie, Mr. Blanc."

"Oh my god."

"You're not going to call me Dave, are you. And it's not that way with us – is it, Connie? I'm a clownish dick, and she loves to hate my guts. That's our thing, our dynamic dynamic."

"The clowns are really going to hate this chicken cordon bleu," Connie said, staring at Dave, sensing their dynamic dynamic shift under the pressure and pulling herself back from the brink. *I am his producer; I produce him; he is my production.* "You'll have to ask what they think about the local food scene."

He smiled. "That'll set them off."

"You two are cute," said August. "But, oh dear, this chicken is tough." Her plastic fork snapped. She yelped and cupped her hands over her face.

"Holy shit," said Dave.

"I'm so sorry, Connie," August said through her fingers in a muffled, tearful voice. "I brought plastic utensils, because I promised to be extra careful, and now look – a fork in my good eye."

Connie froze, said nothing, did nothing. She was too busy mentally recording every detail. Dave seemed to be doing the same. They aligned on the question of journalistic intervention, and neither made a move to help August. She was their true subject, not the clowns. She was the story they were producing. August was their production. And if August was their production, they were hers.

A clown from a neighbouring table jumped up, clutched August's bare shoulders. *"Mademoiselle! Je vais vous aider."* He looked at Dave and Connie in disgust.

"I love clowns," whispered August.

The heroic French clown carried August out of the banquet hall and, as Connie and Dave learned later, placed her gently in an idling taxi which took them to Emergency. The doctor merely prepared new bandages and switched over the eye patch, because August's other eye injury had healed. And now, of course, she enjoys French health care, so their only worry is for her clown.

Connie doesn't produce Dave anymore – he's taken his talents to television – but they still clown around about August often. They raise a glass and drink to her health, then say something like, *We're going to have to drink a lot. Haha. No problem.* They describe the moment she met her clown as a coup de foudre. As opposed to their coming together, which was less thunderbolt and more steady building of campfire by boy scout, stick by stick, waiting for permission to light it, and permission finally granted by August. Sometimes they wonder if they made her up, whether she's a folie à deux. And sometimes they worry about their unscripted future together.

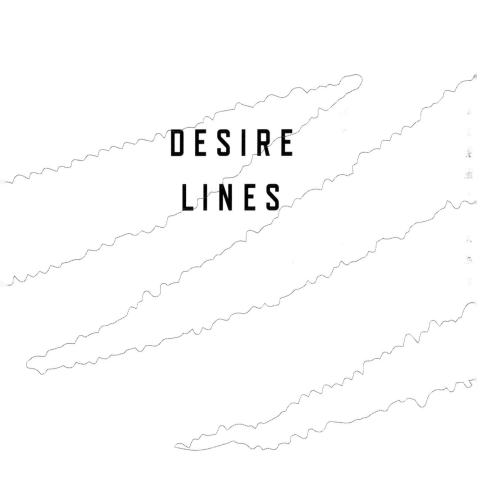

DESIRE LINES

When **Shawn first** arrived to clear out the late Jake Bamford's house, it stank. Under the mice's high-ammonia tang, a middle C of disintegrating newsprint played below his nose, but on day four of the job, as he eats his meatball sandwich at the yellow Formica table in the kitchen, he doesn't notice the smells. Either he's cleaned sufficiently or he's gotten used to them. A mouse skitters in his periphery. Scurrying along their old trails, the mice are exposed; no more cozy burrows in mountains of newspapers, just wide open, eviscerating space. He's caught at least forty so far in snap traps he's set up along their obsessive and self-destructive desire lines. Stupid mice.

In his junk-hauling business, he's encountered hoarding before – this drawer is for empty tape dispensers, that shelf is where you keep the broken clock radios, this stairwell is for twenty years' worth of weekly *Maclean's* magazines. The Formica table was, only a few days ago, piled high, and, apart from the one unsettling exception in the den, every surface in the house was similarly swamped. No, it's not the hoarding that surprises; it's that he kind of likes this guy. Jake Bamford was not your average hoarder. He had discernment.

Consider the locked library upstairs. Left without a key, he took an axe to the door that morning to find an avalanche of good taste behind it: Homer, Tolstoy, Proust, Austen, Borges, Joyce, Hemingway, Carver, Mantel, Munro, numerous editions of Shakespeare. Bamford's daughter will probably want the books – her name is Beatrice, same as his own daughter, Little Bea, who is twelve and perfect – but if not, he might add them to his own collection. If Tina lets him. But having recently bought out his brother, he's got the old barn and farmhouse for storage, so maybe it's not so much a matter of seeking permission as doing what he pleases.

It's Thursday. Tomorrow morning the cleaners come. Saturday's the open house. He's cleared out the basement, main floor, stairs, bathrooms, and half the library and has the rest of the second floor to finish today. On Monday, he took stock and decided to leave the master bedroom and den for last. Bedrooms were almost always his least favourite rooms to clear – too private, too redolent of stale dreams – but this den with its uncluttered desk at its centre gives him the creeps. Why this outpost of cleanliness?

He drops his sandwich as a mouse trap snaps in the living room, and his phone plinks out the first bars of "You're So Cool," signalling a text from Tina. Hans Zimmer's *True Romance* theme once seemed appropriate for his wife's calls and texts, but lately has begun to feel overly optimistic.

Dentist says Bea needs braces ☹

Of course she needs braces. Why should the dental work end now? He texts back a zipper face. He loves emoji more than is reasonable for a grown man with a master's degree in English literature. Maybe he should write his doctoral thesis in emoji. Maybe that way he'd finish.

Wish you'd purchased that dental plan. Mine won't cover it.

He replies with images of a face with a surgical mask and a pair of pliers.

He checks the snap trap. The mouse's split belly reveals a tiny mouse fetus among the guts. "Sorry about that." He tosses the whole mess – mouse, fetus, trap – into the industrial garbage bin outside the front door. Beside it is the storage container where he'll put the books.

I don't want to see any more of your clients' shit in my house. Do NOT bring home one more thing! Unless it's a dental plan.

"You're So Cool" plays again as he's walking back to the kitchen, but there's no new message from Tina. There's a parrot on the kitchen table making a hash of his apple, its body a kaleidoscope of greens and yellows with a patch of blue-grey at its throat, and, pivoting, it flashes red tail feathers. It's alive! Big Bea warned he might find a dead parrot. The bird rasps and raises its wings and produces another faithful rendition of "You're So Cool." A live parrot helps explain the odd noises over the last few days: beeps, scratches, clicks, the doorbell ringing. How has he not seen the bird before now? It must be starving. As if reading his mind, the bird continues ransacking his lunch. He lunges and saves his meatball sandwich. He records a voice memo on his phone. "Protagonist owns pet parrot?"

His novel-in-progress features a writer–junk hauler who finds the dead body of his estranged brother in one of the houses he's emptying. The writer's afraid the police will think he murdered his brother, given their fraught relationship, so he packs the body into a box and wheels him out of the house on a dolly, then drives out of town to their parents' farm and buries him under the barn. The rest of the plot is worked out in his head, more or less, but he needs a good foundation first. There's no point doing anything unless you're going to do it right, and his first chapter needs to be perfect: complex character development, meaningful descriptive passages, realistic and propulsive dialogue, strong verbs, proper punctuation.

Parrot? parrots the parrot from the kitchen table. Is that doubt he hears echoed? A hint of the bird's own incredulity? The only projects he seems able to complete are junk-hauling jobs. He never has enough time for the work he really cares about – his scholarship, his writing. Must change that. But how? Sell the business? To one of those young guys he's hired in the past? They'd ruin his brand. Love's Labour has a reputation. Maybe he's getting ahead of himself. He's been fantasizing about a pseudonym for when the book's published but hasn't settled on one yet. The need for a pseudonym is not because he cares what his brother might read into the characters, but because "Shawn" is too weak and "Diakiw" is impossible.

The parrot clutches the apple core in its claws and flaps over to the clean countertop by the sink. Shawn leans both arms on the table to get a closer look at the bird ripping out the heart of the apple core, scattering seeds over the countertop and onto the floor. The bird makes a sound like a kazoo honk and repeats the single syllable. The bird wheezes the word a third time: *Jake.* Of course! Jake Bamford! The perfect pseudonym. Jake: pow! Bamford: bam! He slams his palm on the table, and the bird flaps to the top of the kitchen cupboards, ducking its head to fit under the ceiling. He *will* finish. He's almost got the first chapter where he wants it. Just has to add the piece about the parrot. He's really starting to like this Jake Bamford. And his parrot.

The daughter will be pleased with him for finding the bird. Big Bea called last week when he was in his tiny, cinder-block office next to the CrossFit, because his third office assistant of the year hadn't shown up for work. "Are you free for a big job? Tight turnaround? I need a house cleared out by next Friday for an open house on Saturday. Can you do it? I'm coming to you."

Big Bea roared up in her vintage Porsche 911 ten minutes later. She tipped over Tina's potted geranium with her oversized purse on the way in the door and, in the relative murk of the office, pushed her sunglasses onto the top of her head. The skin around her eyes was puffy, and she apologized for the plant. "I'm not myself." She squinted at him and glanced around at the clutter. He only saw it when someone else did. "You look like a man who'd understand my dad." She seemed familiar, but he couldn't remember how he knew her. She was an optometrist, like her father. "You may know me from my LogMAR chart." She was attractive, but the lacy bra revealed by a carelessly undone button made him look away. And now he feels a kinship, and wants to honour her dad: discerning reader, parrot owner, holder of his future pseudonym, and father who wisely named his daughter Beatrice. Optometry. Of course! The perfect profession for Little Bea, who aces every class, including science.

He really needs to finish the library, then start work on the bedroom and den. The parrot squawks two syllables that sound like *Postpone*. He sets a quarter-full coffee cup on top of the fridge. A layered phyllo of papers and photographs coats the fridge and freezer doors, and, instead of heading upstairs, he removes powerful, ancient magnets one by one, gathers up all the papers, and spreads them on the table: shopping lists, notices from the city, handwritten letters, bills, symphony ticket stubs from 1987, receipts faded to pricelessness, photographs. One is a black and white of two smiling boys at each end of a pole from which dangle three freshly caught fish.

In a colour photo, a teenaged Beatrice in braces and a pastel sweater smiles behind a man, Bamford presumably, seated at the yellow kitchen table with a birthday cake in front of him, 50 written in icing. He wears a trim mustache, sports coat, bow tie, a green-hued parrot on his shoulder. How old is that bird? Birthday candles illuminate the happy faces in a warm glow, but stacks of newspapers and a pyramid of tin cans loom on the counter behind father and daughter. Wondering who took the picture, Shawn picks out a postcard of the Roman Forum.

Hi Dad, Ancient bits everywhere! The boys here call out Bella, Bella. But don't worry! I can take care of myself. Overnight train to Venice tonight. Can't wait to feed the pigeons and get lost in the maze of streets just like you and mom did. Sorry about mom. She'll come back. Love you. xo, Bea.

He isn't surprised Bamford's wife left him and doesn't doubt Big Bea could take care of herself no matter the situation, no matter her age. He hopes Little Bea will be as self-assured. Voice memo: "Have protagonist remember Venice fondly? His logic as twisted as the streets?" He's always wanted to tour Italy but has never made it happen. He stacks all the papers neatly by estimated date and places them in a small box labelled *Meaningful papers, Fridge.*

The parrot flutters off the cupboard onto the table, hops on top of the box, turns twice, and flaps onto Shawn's shoulder. He flinches but is soothed as claws bunch his work shirt, massaging his trapezius while the bird settles into a comfortable spot. He approaches the stairs gingerly and walks up as if he were balancing a dictionary on his head. At the top he turns into the hallway and passes the bedroom and den without looking in, then steps over the splintered remains of the door he chopped through that morning and into the small library. The parrot pushes off his shoulder, drops onto the broken door, and pecks at the wood.

He shakes his head at the boxes of books already packed. There's no helping it – he'll have to repack. The taxonomy he came up with this morning is no good; the initial sort by form then genre has resulted in several near-empty and half-full boxes. The quirky collection suggests a reader who'll try anything – nonsense verse, Harlequin romances, Michel Houellebecq novels. Difficult to organize. He can't believe how far he is from his deconstructionist grad school past. Imagine Derrida, with his French-intellectual cloud of white hair, applying his theories to the task of dismantling the house of a dead man, packing up a library, tossing books into boxes at random – because a text *participates* in genre but does not *belong* – puffing on his pipe, unconcerned that the next owner of the books will open the boxes to find a meaningless jumble. He'd have to fire Derrida like he had the others.

Shawn pulls on his gloves and unpacks the books. He re-sorts and repacks along geographic lines, secondarily by period – Tolstoy and Chekhov jostle in one box; Sartre and de Beauvoir snuggle in another. He isn't completely satisfied with this new taxonomy because it reveals a cultural bias, but the classification scheme provides some order to the chaos. He's pleased to see Shakespeare get a box of his own. Loving Shakespeare far more than a deconstructionist should was one of the reasons he abandoned his doctoral studies. Plus, the heaps of criticism that grew every day. Just when he thought he could start writing his thesis, he read a new article by some scholar in India, which sent him off in a new direction;

meanings multiplied. Eventually, the theory became too slippery, his thesis advisor retired, and Shawn launched Love's Labour Hauling. He keeps up with Shakespeare scholarship, but Tina is now hassling him to move his research files to the farmhouse. He prefers working on the novel anyway. He isn't sure why he never thought of writing one before. Any dummy can write a novel. And this time he's going to pin meaning to the ground and hold it there even if it kicks and writhes. The first chapter is the tricky part.

"You're So Cool" plays in the paper-dust air. The parrot is nowhere to be seen.

Bea came home with a note from her teacher today. Says she swore at the recess monitor. Whose influence could that be?

Emoji alone cannot handle this reply. *What were the fucking circumstances?* < Swing-set emoji > < Knife emoji >

Some things are just wrong.

Thinking makes it so. < Flag of Denmark emoji >

I'm taking away her phone for a week.

There's logic in this consequence, but he won't go so far as to agree in text or in emoji and puts his phone back in his pocket. Then it trembles and launches into "Crazy" by Gnarls Barkley, the first song he and Bea both loved together.

"Hi Bea. I thought Mom was taking away your phone."

"She is. It's like I'm in jail and this is my only phone call. You should feel special."

"I always do when you call, Bea-Bea, but what's this I hear?" He pictures Bea's dramatic, preteen eye roll for her mother's benefit and smiles.

"Dad, it was so unfair. I was just quoting that awesome line from *Kill Bill: Volume 1*, you know the one where Lucy

Liu's on the table and she holds up that guy's head." She whisper-shouts the character's menacing words very impressively, emphasizing "now's the fucking time," and Tina in the background says, *What!* "I was just quoting! Because no one else has seen the movie yet, but they all want to see it now. *Kill Bill*'s a classic. Right, Dad?"

"Yes, it is, but please don't make me regret our first annual Daddy-Daughter Tarantino Film Festival. I don't want it to be our last, so let's keep those lines between us, okay?"

"But Dad —"

"I know, life's not fair. Also context dependent, so love and defend that movie, just don't quote from it in front of your mother or at school. Love you."

"Fine. Love you too."

The doorbell rings, and he looks down at the parrot sorting through the splinters that lie all around the library's door. The bird nods, flashes red, and *ding-dongs* again. Voice memo: "Protagonist's parrot quotes Tarantino lines?"

It's midnight and Shawn leans against the den's door frame, exhausted but awake thanks to caffeine. His arms feel weighted, like he has dumbbells hanging from his wrists, and his back aches beneath the support belt. He's finally too tired to be freaked out by the den and its weirdly uncluttered desk, the oasis of order within a desert of chaos. He adjusts his dust mask and steps in. The whole room, with the exception of the desk, is piled to eye level in messy, overlapping stacks of periodicals and loose papers. He starts by widening the path to the desk, lifting crumbling newsprint into boxes, and wades into the room deep enough to reach the parrot's cage teetering on top of a pile. The bird pecks on another pile, topped with a leaking bag of birdseed. From underneath layers of paper, he excavates twelve typewriters, six computer monitors, seven hard drives, five printers, and ten keyboards – along with associated hardware – and uncovers two office chairs, one leather club chair, eleven task lamps, and reams of paper still in wrappers, while the small stuff sifts onto the floor. Finally, he shovels up empty ink cartridges, expended typewriter ribbon, and enough HB pencils to satisfy a grade one school supply list.

At two o'clock, he pulls down his dust mask and perches on the edge of the desk for a break, pouring himself a cup of coffee from his Thermos. From behind him, he hears an echo of the splash of coffee filling a cup. "Let's get you some water." He holds out his hand and the parrot hops onto it and climbs up his arm. In the bathroom, he fills the Thermos lid with water and looks up at the mirror: he's wan beside the parrot's vibrant greens and yellows, and the blue-grey around the bird's throat matches the bags under his eyes. Starting to look like an old man. As if in tactful agreement, the parrot nods slightly and looks away. Back in the den, he sets the Thermos lid in front of the parrot. It dips its beak into the water several times, darting its strange black tongue back and forth, then steps back, spreads its wings in a satisfied stretch, and honks, *Jake.* Wings snug into body, the bird bobs in the direction of the office chair.

"Don't mind if I do." He flops into the chair. The armrests are set at the perfect height. He leans back and puts his feet up on the large oak desk with its laptop, task lamp, and printer. What's inside? He takes his feet off and opens the wide front drawer. Inside is a thesaurus and several red felt-tipped pens, his favourite brand, and his preferred dictionary, with select words underlined in red ink. *Jake*, squawks the bird. Again, he approves of the dead man's choices and anxiety carbonates his blood.

On the left side of the desk are three deep drawers. The top one is stacked with sheaves of paper fastened with paper clips. He picks out the topmost sheaf. The heading on the first page is *Untitled, Chapter 1.* He reads. It's about a writer-optometrist who finds the dead body of his brother in his office, an owl-eyed phoropter pinning him to the examination chair. The optometrist is being framed for the murder and panics.

Jake, shrieks the parrot.

He grabs a sheaf from the middle of the pile and finds the same untitled first chapter with minor variations. In this version, the brother is buried in a community garden, rather than the backyard, and the optometrist wears brown coveralls for the job, not khaki pants and a pale-blue shirt. He flips through version after version of the same chapter, all minutely edited with fine, felt-tipped pen. Bloody with corrections. In the bottom version, the protagonist finds a parrot perched on the dead brother's forehead, pecking at his eyes; these sentences are so cross-hatched in red ink that, in places, the page is blurred and torn.

Fizzy blood surges through his veins. Hot with shame for Bamford and for himself, he dreads opening the second drawer, but he does anyway. More drafts of *Untitled, Chapter 1,* the only difference being these printouts have perforated edges. He remembers his undergrad essays manifesting boisterously, line by line from a dot-matrix printer. In the third drawer, he finds typewritten drafts of the same chapter with rust spots under the paper clips. Blackness edges in on his vision as he unfolds the laptop. An open document appears on the screen, the same untitled chapter. Some idea of himself tears, cross-hatched and inked through.

Dizzy, he stumbles from the den into the bedroom and drops onto the edge of Bamford's stripped bed. His mind turns and overturns questions. Who is he? Who was Jake Bamford? Why can't they finish anything? Why can't they get rid of anything? What's he supposed to do? He looks around the bedroom for answers: at the low, long teak dresser; the Eames-style reading chair; the spare, tasteful space that only hours ago was piled high with clutter.

The parrot backs into the room, dragging a sheaf of papers. Shawn cants sideways and tucks up his legs as the bird tears at the chapter, reducing it to bits and strips. The parrot has the right idea.

A sprung snap trap. Another snap. He hopes the sound is coming from the parrot. He's not sure he can face any more eviscerated mice. What did they do to deserve this slaughter? Plus, he needs to go back to sleep to resolve the baroque set of problems his last dream posed. It involved the Beas somehow. He gives up and reaches for the coffee cup on the bedside table. The coffee has evaporated overnight and all that's left is a dry, unsettling residue. He's awake with a dryness in his mouth and a headache reminiscent of a hangover. Signs of being alive. He is not this man, Jake Bamford, despite their strange affinities. Jake Bamford is dead along with his unfinished novel. The sad, mired writer he uncovered the night before is not him, not yet, only a pseudonym, one possible identity.

Maybe as a result of the dream, maybe a result of rest and the parrot's example, the answer has come. What he's supposed to do.

Before the cleaners arrive, he clears the rest of the office in a rush of industry, sending the drafts of *Untitled, Chapter 1* through the working shredder he found yesterday, while the parrot expertly copies its whir. Love's Labour saved him from academia. It bought an engagement ring for Tina. It physically exhausted him, kept him fit. Meant he was completing at least some projects to his satisfaction. It brought order to his life; paid for sweet, weak-toothed Bea's extensive dental care; bought out his brother's share of the farm. And it would pay for this house, the bones of which are beautiful and sturdy, a place to create new desire lines, a place from which to respect – or at least not forget – the old ones. The library can be Bea's bedroom where her dreams will be visited by literary ghosts: Puck appearing as class clown; Ahab in the role of fanatical soccer coach; Elizabeth Bennet, snarky best friend; Nick Adams, dreamy new guy at school with the haunted eyes. Life feels like a fiction, maybe even a literary joke, but he knows how to derive meaning from a text. He knows what to do now.

When Big Bea arrives with the real estate agent around noon, he resists the urge to run over and hug this version of his own grown daughter. Because of her T-shirt, messy ponytail, and sad smile at the house's transformation, she seems still not herself – he imagines her in other contexts, other fictions. With two swords in a Tarantino film, leaping nimbly down a long boardroom table, aiming to decapitate.

.

LIKE THE GIRL SHE IMAGINES

They play their card games in the common room of Aspen Grove. Usually, it's while Tina talks to the aides and tidies her father's room, watering the plants and arranging the fresh flowers she brings, but she couldn't make it tonight so Shawn's here all alone. That may be why he's more anxious than usual. Or it may be because he hasn't lost a game against his father-in-law in weeks.

They walk slowly away from Manfred's room between walls the colour of desert sand. The old guy won't accept help, nor will he use his wheelchair, so the pace is agonizing as he grips the handrails at every step and wheezes while Shawn turns inside out with frustration. He remembers this feeling from when Bea was little. *Noooo, Daddy, I can do it myself! Stop it!* Who knew he would feel a parent's concern and impatience with this old man?

"*Bonjour*, Manny," says Charlotte, a fellow resident, as they take their usual seats at the card table near the window. Manfred replies with something under his breath that Shawn can't understand and chooses to ignore. Charlotte witnesses all of their games, and here she is again tonight, doing a new puzzle. Her hair is freshly dyed, a Betty-Boop black, with eyebrows painted to match. Red lipstick is bleeding into her upper lip. On her cheeks are matching spots of colour.

"Hello, Charlotte. How's the puzzle coming?"

"A beauty. Notre-Dame cathedral. Before the fire, *bien sûr. Je me souviens de Paris au printemps. Quelle beauté.*" She shakes her head.

"Yes, very beautiful."

When he hears Manfred start to cough, he hopes the episode will be bad enough to put the old man back in his room. But Manfred pulls a stained hanky out of his pocket, coughs one last time and wipes his mouth.

Shawn sets up the cribbage board. "How's your buddy, McLean, McLeod, I can't —"

"McDead is how he is."

He pauses from shuffling the deck. "I'm sorry to hear that."

"If you haven't heard, Shawn-boy, people come here to die."

He concentrates on dealing the cards, catches a draft of lavender coming from Charlotte's direction.

"Didn't you enjoy playing cards with him?" He knocks twice on the top of the deck. A few cards flip as Manfred's skeletal hand shakes through a sloppy cut. "That's okay, Dad. Let me."

"Goddamn hands. Beat him all the time if that's what you mean."

"I liked the old guy. Funny. Every time I saw him he'd say, 'You're the writer? Have I got a story for you.' Then he'd tell me a joke. 'Write that down, now, you can have it.'"

"Funny, huh." Manfred arranges and rearranges the cards in his hand, slowly picking up the ones he drops, refusing to use the plastic holders provided by the home. He glares at the cards and finally slaps one onto the table. "Ten."

Shawn wins the first hand by a wide margin. He doesn't count many points during the game — successfully avoiding pegging on pairs, fifteens, and thirty-ones — but his hand adds up to a decent eight despite his efforts to break it up, and it's his crib.

"Fifteen two, four, two runs for ten, and a pair for twelve," he says. "Wow, lucky crib."

His opponent grunts and starts shuffling. Cards slide across and under the table, but when Shawn sees a five leak from the old man's fingers and slip under the easy chair, he doesn't retrieve it. One less winning card to find in his hand.

"Losing it upstairs." Manfred taps his head with the card and then smacks it down. "Eight."

"Who? Um, sixteen for two."

"McLean. Twenty-one."

"Dad? Are you sure you want to play that one? Okay, okay. Thirty-one for two. Maybe that's why he wasn't playing so —"

"That's a load of shit. Once a card player; always a card player."

"Well, that's true. Do you remember when I was first dating Tina? All those games at your dining room table? I embarrassed her. She brings home this guy who doesn't even know tricks and trump. What kind of a boyfriend is that, right? Your turn."

"The wife thought you were quite something. Ten."

"Marie was very kind. Twenty."

"With your university degrees. Thirty."

"Thirty-one for two. Yes, and I don't even know tricks and trump." He knows he could deliberately play even worse, but Manfred is sharp. It would be noticed. This hand he counts more points despite Manfred's having the crib, and deals again. They play in silence for a while. Just counting points aloud.

"She was a terrible cook, that woman."

"What?"

"I get better food here."

"Do you mean Marie?"

"Who else? Our private chef? Yes, Marie."

When Shawn thinks of Marie, he thinks of her in the kitchen or the garden. Those were her spaces. Whenever she wasn't in one of those spaces, she seemed adrift, uncertain, as if she were in a hotel room. While having coffee in the living room, for instance, she might pick up a figurine and say, "Is this ours? Where did we get this?" Tina would reply, "Mom, that's been on the piano since I painted it in grade two. You dust it every week." This was well before the real dementia set in. "Oh, what a lovely job you did, dear. Always so precise, you were. Let me get us some more cookies." Then she'd flee to her kitchen.

"Where's Tina?"

"I told you, Dad. She's at the library board meeting tonight. Some program went sideways. Bea's at soccer practice."

In truth, Bea's at home, purportedly studying for a math test. Now that she is old enough to stay home alone, she chooses that over her grandad. In the next hand, he donates a pair of sixes to Manfred's crib, but pegs six points and counts nine in his hand. Manfred counts a lousy three in his hand and looks at his crib. "A pair for two. Jesus. You still don't know what you're doing. You gave me a pair." He coughs and fumbles his peg, losing it somewhere in his pajamas.

"Let's just use one of the green ones, Dad." He takes the opportunity to give his father-in-law a few extra points.

"Are you feeling sorry for me? Goddamnit!"

The game continues for another few hands until Shawn's little blue pegs are well ahead of Manfred's red and green. He's going to skunk the old man if he's not careful.

As he shuffles the deck for a seventh hand, Manfred says, "She could have done better."

"Who?"

"Tina."

He stops shuffling and examines his father-in-law: yellowish, rheumy eyes; crumpled, grey face; crooked hands; oversized, stained pajamas and housecoat on his wire clothes hanger of a body. Still has that thick head of white hair, though.

In the silence, Charlotte asks, "*Qu'est-ce qui se passe, mes gars?* Who's winning? Manny, judging by all that grumbling, I'm guessing that you've had some *malchance.*"

"None of your goddamned business."

"Dad! I'm sorry, Charlotte. He didn't mean that."

"*Je comprends.* I've had some bad luck in my life."

"That's not bad luck."

"Manny, if you lose, this will be the, what," Charlotte counts on her fingers and looks up at the ceiling, "tenth game in a row?"

"He'll come back this time. Right, Dad? Back to your old self, eh?"

"So, this *malchance* is new, Manny? You've been a lucky man? Not like my *pauvres* husbands. Died before their time, every one."

"Whore."

"Dad! Oh my god, I am so sorry, Charlotte. Game's over, all right?"

"*Mais non, continuez.*" Charlotte pushes her chair away from the puzzle, and Shawn, rushing over, holds her elbow as she stands. "I'm off. A girl needs her beauty sleep."

As he helps her to the hallway, he hears Manfred say, "Shawn? Where are you?" He turns and, noticing her silk scarf dragging on the floor, picks it up and lays it over her arm.

"Are you okay?" he asks when out of earshot. "I can't apologize enough. I don't know what's got into him."

"*Mon chéri*, if I let that bother me? No. I'm an expert at outlasting men. You go back to your game."

"I think we're done with cards for tonight."

"Please finish. I insist."

"I can't seem to lose. Only now, when he's dying. It's terrible."

She looks at him with her huge, black-ringed eyes and says, "Manny is right, you know. People come here to die. You too?"

He laughs, a bark echoing along the polished surfaces of the corridor. Taking a step back, he bows, weirdly gallant, and in his high-school French says, "*Pas encore, mademoiselle.*" He offers her his arm again. "Do you need help to your room?"

"*Non, merci.*" She tosses the long end of her scarf over her shoulder, carefree and confident like the girl she imagines she is in Paris.

He walks back to the common room, where he will sit and deal another hand.

ACKNOWLEDGEMENTS

Earlier versions of some of these stories appeared in *Prairie Fire*, *PRISM international*, *The Malahat Review*, *The New Quarterly*, *subTerrain*, *Grain*, and *paperplates*. Thank you to the editors, staff, readers, and funders of these publications.

Thank you to Elizabeth Philips, Caroline Walker, and JoAnn McCaig of Thistledown Press and to Michael Kenyon, the brilliant editor of this book.

Thank you to the Saskatchewan Writers' Guild. Special thanks for the advice and encouragement to my SWG mentor, Sylvia Legris.

Thank you to the Saskatoon Public Library for its Writer in Residence program.

Thank you to the ENG 366.3 class and the terrific writer and teacher, Guy Vanderhaeghe.

Thank you to my writing group pals, past and present, and, in particular, to Jenny Ryan, Melanie Cole, and Ann Foster.

Finally, thank you to my family.

PHOTO CREDIT: KATE MYROL

Theressa Slind is a writer and librarian based in Saskatoon. Her fiction has appeared in *Grain, Prairie Fire, The Malahat Review, The New Quarterly,* and elsewhere. *Only If We're Caught* is her first book.